Faster than the Swords

A novel about the Rebecca Riots in the Tywi valley, summer 1843

Myrddin ap Dafydd

translated from the Welsh by Susan Walton

Gwasg Carreg Gwalch

First published in Welsh as *Rhedeg yn Gynt na'r Cleddyfau*, 2021
Published in English: 2022

ISBN: 978-1-84527-884-7

CYNGOR LLYFRAU CYMRU
BOOKS COUNCIL of WALES

Published with the financial support of the
Books Council of Wales

Cover design: Siôn Ilar
Maps: Alison Davies

Published by Gwasg Carreg Gwalch,
12 Iard yr Orsaf, Llanrwst, Wales LL26 0EH
tel: 01492 642031
email: books@carreg-gwalch.cymru
website: www.carreg-gwalch.cymru

Published and printed in Wales

Presented in memory
of Jac from the Plough Inn,
who engendered the spirit of
Beca in our family

Special thanks
– to Ieuan Jones, local historian of Llandeilo, and Heddyr Gregory for a wealth of local knowledge
– to Alun Jones, Llio Elenid and Anwen Pierce for helpful suggestions, additional information and advice on the dialect.

The Main Characters

Tafarn y Wawr family, Llangadog

Brython Rees – father, publican, owner of a few fields and a
horse and cart

Tegwen Rees – mother, publican's wife

Elin Rees – daughter, 15 years old, works in her parents' pub

Gwyndaf Rees – son, 15 years old, works in his parents' pub

Gwladys Rees – Brython's sister, deceased

Romani family on Coed yr Arlwydd Common

Jorjo Lee – father, basket-maker and casual farm labourer

Mari Lee – mother, basket-maker

Tom Lee – son, 18 years old, basket-maker and casual farm
labourer

Anna Lee – daughter, 15 years old, basket-maker

Blacksmith's family, Carreg Sawdde Common

Llew Lewis – blacksmith

Dan Dowlais – son, 30 years old, blacksmith

Plough Inn family, Rhosmaen

Jac Griffiths – father, innkeeper and brewer

Leisa Griffiths – mother, innkeeper's wife

Ann Griffiths – daughter, 20 years old, works in her parents' inn

Iori Griffiths – son, 17 years old, works in the stables of the
King's Head, Llandeilo

Pont Carreg Sawdde toll-house family

Simon Powell – father, toll-keeper and wearer of a bowler hat

Nona Powell – mother, toll-keeper's wife

Rachel, Mei, Dafy – their children

Pont Goch Cottage family

Edryd Morgan – forester and worker at Melin-y-cwm sawmill

Nest Morgan – Edryd's wife

Other characters

Bishop – steward of Newton House, Dinefwr Park

Colonel Love – officer in charge of over 2,000 soldiers in
West Wales during the Rebecca Riots

Richard Chandler – parish beadle for Llangadog; collector of
the church rate and tithes

Dylan Lloyd – local reporter for the *Carmarthen Journal*, the
weekly newspaper for Carmarthen and Carmarthenshire

Thomas Campbell Foster – reporter for *The Times* of London

The man in the black cravat – who is everywhere and nowhere

Romani words used in the story

    diklo = scarf

    divvus = day

    dordi! = blimey!

    mingries = police

    pani = water

    ped = walk

    shushi = rabbit

    waffadi = bad

Prologue

Sawdde valley, Llangadog, Sunday night, 25 June 1843

The white pony is lame, and he's getting worse.

"Woah, Dicw," says Jorjo, who is walking alongside him, leading him by his bridle. "Let's have another look at that painful hoof of yours."

Tom and Anna turn back to see what's wrong, and watch their father leaning across the horse's leg. They're fed up with the slow pace and are dying to get to the common in the woods.

"Are we going to get to Coed yr Arlwydd before nightfall, Tada?" asks Anna.

"Can he carry on?" Tom asks, showing more concern for the horse than his sister had.

"It's this shoe that's come loose." Jorjo shows his son the hoof. "A stone has worked its way between the shoe and the hoof and it's rubbed against the softer part. That's what's caused the injury, you see. He needs a rest."

"But it's almost dark," Anna says.

"It's midsummer. It never gets properly dark at this time of year," says Mari Lee, her mother, handing Jorjo a dark-coloured bottle. "Put a drop of rosemary oil on it to keep it clean."

Jorjo gently rubs a few drops of oil into the troublesome hoof before straightening up.

"Better weather this year, thank goodness," he says. "Do

8

you remember two years ago? The river Sawdde was in flood here and the ford was impassable. We had to camp on the common on this side of the river."

"There was a poor harvest," says Mari Lee. "That year the harvest couldn't sustain the farmers."

"It wasn't the same, though, on the other common, was it?" Anna says. "Oh, I love it in the woods, and having the place to ourselves. It's not the same thing down the valley, with other families camped there."

"Maybe not, but the common is just that – a field for everyone. It's nice to have company and a chat sometimes," says Mari Lee.

"And a story and a sing-song," adds Jorjo, grinning broadly, his white teeth sparkling in his tanned face.

"But two years ago it was too wet to think of making a fire or sitting out in one big gang late into the night," Anna says.

"Are we alright to go on, Tada?" Tom asks.

"If we go steady, very steady," Jorjo answers. "We're not far from the ford. Dicw can stand a while in the river to cool that hoof before climbing the hill up to the wood."

"How about easing his load a bit?" Mari Lee suggests. "We could carry the small chest, the tent and the hazel poles. An empty cart would be lighter for him."

"Dicw's strong enough," Jorjo says. "But maybe you're right. It's not far for us to carry the heaviest things."

Jorjo goes round to the back of the cart and pulls off a small chest, which he shoulders. Tom lifts the tent canvas and carries it, and Anna grabs the hazel poles that form the tent's frame. Mari Lee takes the big, black cooking pot and slots it over her arm.

After they have travelled on a while, the family reach the cottage of Pen-y-bont Sawdde and they can see the trees of Coed yr Arlwydd on the slope rising from the other side of the river.

"We're so close!" says Anna. "Can we cross the Sawdde here?"

"The cart has to go through the ford," says Jorjo. "The riverbed is tricky because the ford has been left to its own devices since they built the new bridge – Pont Carreg Sawdde – further down."

"But there must have been a bridge here at one time," Tom says.

"Yes, there was," Jorjo replies. "But it was really old. Ancient, in fact. It got swept away in a big flood years ago, and there's been no bridge here since. But the name of the farm over the other side of the river is still Pen-y-bont, as if there was still a pont here."

"And we always go through the old ford," says Mari Lee. "There's a turnpike gate on the bridge and another barrier between Pont Carreg Sawdde and Coed yr Arlwydd."

Just then, the family hears the sound of a bugle. Three notes, the last of which is held for a long time.

"Dragoons," Jorjo says. "Stay where you are. Get between the cart and the hedge ..."

From Pen-y-bont Sawdde, there is a quarter of a mile of straight road towards Llangadog. The family can see more than twenty Dragoons, in their dark blue uniforms and high, plumed hats, appearing out of the late evening gloom. They are mounted on large horses and are moving away from the village. They hear a harsh voice shouting commands, and see the gleam of long swords as the soldiers draw them from their scabbards. They all hold their swords at the same angle, and then the harsh voice comes again. The horses start to gallop towards them.

"Don't move a muscle," Jorjo warns. "Stay between the cart and the hedge. Whatever you do, don't try and run faster than the swords ..."

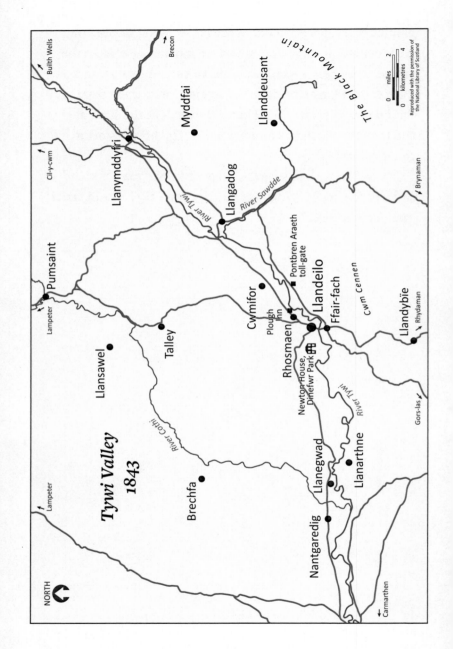

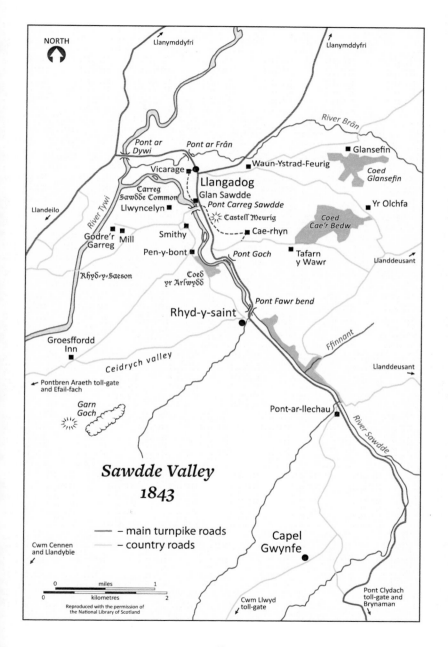

NORTH

Llanymddyfri

Llanymddyfri

River Brân

Glansefin

Coed
Glansefin

Pont ar
Dywi

Pont ar Frân

Waun-Ystrad-Feurig

Vicarage

Llangadog

Carreg
Sawdde Common

Glan Sawdde

Pont Carreg Sawdde

Yr Olchfa

Llwyncelyn

Castell Meurig

Coed
Cae'r Bedw

Llandeilo

River Tywi

Smithy

Cae-rhyn

Godre'r
Garreg

Mill

Pen-y-bont

Pont Goch

Tafarn
y Wawr

Llanddeusant

Rhyd-y-Saeson

Coed
pr Arlwydd

Pont Fawr bend

Rhyd-y-saint

Groesffordd
Inn

Ceidrych valley

Ffinnant

Llanddeusant

Pontbren Araeth toll-gate
and Efail-fach

Garn
Goch

Pont-ar-llechau

River Sawdde

Sawdde Valley
1843

— main turnpike roads
— country roads

Capel
Gwynfe

Cwm Cennen
and Llandybïe

0   miles   1
0   kilometres   2

Reproduced with the permission of
the National Library of Scotland

Cwm Llwyd
toll-gate

Pont Clydach
toll-gate and
Brynaman

13

Chapter 1

Major William Parlby is not in a good mood. All day he's been going around looking like thunder.

He and his cavalry – the 4th Light Dragoons – are leading the charge against the so-called Daughters of Rebecca, after travelling at full speed in oppressive heat to Carmarthen the previous Monday. Four or five thousand people had been parading through the town's main streets under a banner adorned with some nonsense in Welsh about 'Justice'.

That day, the Major and his Dragoons had galloped from Cross Hands after a messenger had been sent post-haste to say that folk were attacking the town of Carmarthen. When they'd reached the town, its narrow streets were thronged with people, and crowds were surging forward to attack the workhouse, shouting that the dark building was the Bastille! Whatever next – beheading the queen and her consort? This rabble were as dangerous as the hordes of barbarians in Paris at the time of the French Revolution! However, in Carmarthen the cold steel of the Dragoons had cooled them down. In no time at all, people had scattered over the fields and through the hedges, away into the countryside.

But they'd failed to capture that rascal in the yellow wig, the one wearing women's clothes and riding a white horse. He that was referred to as 'Beca' and who was leading the whole thing. It was he who dressed up like an old woman and took his crowds of 'daughters' with him to smash up the toll-gates with sledgehammers and axes, and even by burning. He, who would be in Llanfihangel-ar-arth one night, St Clears a few nights later, then in Cardigan on the coast the next, before striking unexpectedly soon afterwards in some village far inland. And with two or three hundred following him each time! It should be pretty straightforward to find such a multitude making mischief so openly, what with the noise of weapons being fired and their horns blaring. Catching that ringleader on the white horse would do the trick, and then string him up. No messing about.

Well, at least they'd bloodied their long sabres in Carmarthen. The Dragoons' swords had sliced through clothes and flesh as if they had been paper. There was no doubt, thinks William Parlby, that the pools of blood in the street had brought the crowd to their senses pretty sharpish.

But the one mounted on the white horse had gathered the rioters back together and got them worked up enough to attack another gate – that very same night! In the full knowledge that there were fifty cavalrymen with swift horses and deadly weapons billeted in Carmarthen.

Then, at four o'clock in the afternoon the following day, Beca's army had gathered in a village near St Clears. In broad daylight! 'She' was there, of course, on her white horse, resplendent in her fabulous attire, and that night the gates at either end of St Clears were destroyed. For ten hours they'd rioted – and where was the command for the Dragoons to attack? But at the very same time, other gangs were destroying the gates at Nantgaredig and Dryslwyn bridge, twenty miles away.

It was clear that more soldiers were needed to restore order to such a lawless country. Last Friday, Colonel James Frederick Love and one hundred and fifty foot soldiers had arrived in Carmarthen; they are being accommodated in the workhouse. Colonel Love has been appointed commander of all troops within the area of unrest, including regiments in Pembroke Dock, Cardigan, Newcastle Emlyn, St Clears and Carmarthen – over nine hundred soldiers. And there's talk of doubling that number soon. It's the only way to ensure peace – let the army take over and give them free rein.

But what did Colonel Love go and do today? Send half his cavalrymen up the Tywi valley, of all places. A Colonel Trevor is afraid his grand house in the estate at Dinefwr Park will be targeted by the woman on the white horse and her unruly children. But all was calm when they arrived at Llandeilo and took a little refreshment at the Cawdor Hotel. Love had sent his best soldiers far from the troublesome areas – and that wasn't the end of it.

"Onwards towards Llanymddyfri and cross Pont ar Dywi to Llangadog." That was the order to the Dragoons. "Keep an eye on the road over from the village to the Black Mountain – there are a lot of toll-gates in the area because there's a fair amount of traffic for farmers to the north of the county that comes over the Black Mountain."

So here they are, in the middle of this peaceful valley. A toot on the bugle as they approach Pont ar Dywi and a shout of "Open the gate for Her Majesty's Dragoons!" The only excitement the soldiers see is the gatekeeper, scared to death and racing to open the gate, before bowing low to the horses and the soldiers.

The villagers in their houses hear the sound of galloping hoofs along the road over the meadows, across the bridge that spans the river Brân and past the church to the square and the Castle Hotel. The men then proceed straight onwards, up the Sawdde valley, reaching another toll-gate before arriving at the old castle, Castell Meurig. The bugle is sounded again and the harsh voice of the Major orders: "Open the gate for Her Majesty's Dragoons."

The same response. On they go. A slight curve in the road, and then a straight stretch for a quarter of a mile.

And what does the Major spot in the distance? He squints, and looks again ...

"By Jove! A white horse ... Draw. Swords. Charge! Charge!"

The galloping horses cover the quarter of a mile of road in seconds, every soldier with his right arm fully extended – the long blade of every sword ready to impale.

Jorjo and his family stand like statues. Dicw starts to fidget, but his owner clasps the white pony's bridle tight. In no time at all, a wall of swords has closed in round the gypsy family.

The Major realises immediately that this isn't the white horse and the dressed-up man they are hunting, but he isn't about to lose face. He starts firing questions at the family.

"What are you doing on the highway this time of night?"

"Long *siwrnai*. Long *ped*. Walk long over hills," Jorjo tries to explain as best he can, jumbling up Welsh and Romani with his faltering English.

He points towards the hills at the end of the Tywi valley. His family had been at a horse fair at Llanybydder a month ago and had sold their old donkey and bought a pony for the first time. It's a strong pony, too, but much smaller than the army horses, of course. They have roamed along their favourite tracks and camped at their favourite stopping places – over Mynydd Pencarreg to Rhydcymerau, then along the drover's route, keeping to the high ground over Mynydd Llansadwrn towards Cil-y-cwm. Avoiding the roads to Llanymddyfri – apart from on fair day – and over the shoulder of Mynydd Myddfai towards Llanddeusant and across the moors to Llangadog. But Jorjo isn't about to try to explain all this to the Major.

"Where are you heading?"

Jorjo points to the wood on the other side of the river, without saying exactly where.

"*Comin,*" he says. That word means that they have a right to go there and there is a firmness in his voice.

"Some sort of a gyppo gathering, is it?" The Major had caught sight of the carts and ponies and families camped on the common on the other side of Pont Carreg Sawdde as they had galloped by. There was no mistaking the contempt in his voice.

"Llandeilo *ffair.* Three *divvus* – three days," says Jorjo.

"Just what we want," snorts William Parlby. "Another excuse to go wild in the town. Sheath your sabres, soldiers. Fall back in order."

While the cavalrymen are reorganising themselves into an orderly company, two by two, the Major turns back to the family.

"It's obvious you don't belong here, but you could be useful while you're on my patch. You will have heard about Rebecca and her Daughters, whom the people hereabouts call 'Beca'. There is a fifty-pound reward for information that will lead to a conviction of anyone connected in any way with these atrocities. Fifty pounds! You could buy a real horse and a real cart with that, and the whole family could live like kings for years!"

"Yes ..."

"Yes – SIR!" barks the officer.

"Yessir."

"Remember – keep your eyes open when you're out poaching during the night. Oh, I know what your lot are up to. Don't withhold information from the authorities. I'll be watching you. Keep your eyes peeled and your nose clean – if that's at all possible for you people."

And with that, he turns his black horse's head and leads his troops up the Sawdde valley.

"A black horse for a black mood," says Mari Lee.

"Let's get through the ford," Jorjo says, and all four walk towards the river without another word.

Jorjo steps into the river in front of Dicw and turns to encourage the horse to follow.

"Tom, you stand beside one wheel of the cart and be ready to turn it with a bit of a shove to help Dicw pull it. Mari and Anna – you do the same with the other wheel."

The white pony hesitates before putting his painful front hoof in the water but, with Jorjo's encouragement, he moves forward. Jorjo lets him have a drink from the river first. Then he stands right in front of him, avoiding looking him straight in the eye. He holds his head down and pushes his forehead now and again against the side of the horse's head, at the same time whispering gentle words and slowly pulling him forward by his bridle. Dicw gains confidence, and although the icy water stabs at his injury, he continues forward with small steps.

"Now then, put some weight behind that wheel ... and one more step, Dicw ... and there we go."

The riverbed is stony. Red stones, some of which are pretty rough, despite their being in the water for goodness knows how long. Smooth stones would have been dangerous to both the horse and its load. Thank goodness for the Sawdde stones, thinks Jorjo. Step by step, they reach the middle of the river. The water level is only knee-deep, but it's fast-flowing and every step has to be considered.

Before long, all four of them, and the horse and cart are safely in the Pen-y-bont meadow. The family quietly follows the river bank and then heads for the road that climbs Coed yr Arlwydd hill.

"Tom, you go ahead with the pail and the cooking pot. We'll be slow coming up the hill. Do you remember where the spring is?"

"Top corner of the clearing, where the hazel grows."

"Good lad, Tom. You go ahead too, Anna, and take the hazel frame for the tent to the small clearing ..."

"I'll come with you," says Mari, taking the canvas sheeting from her husband and hoisting it onto her shoulder. "I'll be pleased to see our midsummer common."

Once left alone on the hill with the pony and cart, Jorjo hears three notes sounding once more, further up the narrow, wooded valley. The Pont-ar-llechau Gate, the gypsy thinks. Those soldiers are going right the way to the Black Mountain gates to make sure the Daughters of Rebecca aren't abroad tonight.

When man and horse arrive at the clearing, a fire has been lit, the smoke rising, and the bender is taking shape over its frame of hazel poles.

Over on the other side of the valley, a brother and sister are walking home up a path through some fields, after visiting their neighbours at Pont Goch Cottage. They both look at the view from the hillside and notice a ribbon of blue smoke rising above the branches of Coed yr Arlwydd.

"They're back," she says to her brother.

Chapter 2

At the breakfast table the next morning their father asks, "How were they in Pont Goch Cottage last night?"

"Edryd Morgan was out in the farmyard and he said he was going to start the haymaking next week," Elin replies.

"But he was hopping about the place like a one-legged crow," Gwyndaf, her twin, says. "He'll never be able to swing a scythe out in the fields like that."

"No, he's not well at all," Elin agrees.

"He certainly wasn't able to rest his leg when it should have been mending," says Gwyndaf.

"He's paying the price today," Brython Rees, her father, says. "Breaking your leg is no small matter."

"But there was no one to help and the work had to be done," Elin explains. "I'm worried about Nest Morgan too. She's worried that he won't get his work back in the sawmill. She said that Chandler, the church beadle, had been there the other day asking for tithe money and the parish rate. You know what he's like."

"They were supposed to pay the church last spring," Gwyndaf says. "But he had his accident in March ..."

"They've got to pay the estate the rent on the cottage the same month, too," adds Elin. "They're still scraping pennies together to try and settle that bill, Nest told me."

"Goodness me," says their father, "they really poured their

hearts out to you, didn't they! It's not like those two to complain about their lot, either."

He looks across the table at the twins sitting on the other side, and can see that they both sympathise wholeheartedly with the couple at Pont Goch Cottage.

"They're not far off desperation," Elin says gravely.

Silence falls on the breakfast table at Tafarn y Wawr. There, in the kitchen, they can see that the sun is already high in the sky, pouring light through the windows at the front of the old inn. It is situated on the shoulder of a hill above the Sawdde valley and faces east, towards the Black Mountain and the old drovers' road towards Mynydd Epynt. It is the last inn for miles, and from August onwards it will be busy with the drovers who walk herds of cattle and sheep from the Tywi valley and West Wales over Offa's Dyke to the markets in England. The inn has three hayfields; those will soon be cut as feed for the animals when they stay overnight before the big push over the uplands. An old barn in the yard of the inn serves to house the lads helping on the drove. The drovers themselves, of course, sleep in a proper bed in the bedroom of the inn.

"The Lee family are back in Coed yr Arlwydd," Elin says, more brightly.

"We saw smoke from their fire late last night," says Gwyndaf.

"Llandeilo Fair," says Brython. "They never miss it. Their hazel baskets are bound to sell well, as usual."

Every November, the Lee family would call at Coed yr

Arlwydd to cut hazel rods and bend them into the ribs of baskets big enough to be carried with two hands. Then, just ahead of the fair, they would cut young hazel wands to weave round these, creating the base and sides of the circular baskets used for collecting potatoes and fruit during the harvest, and for carrying clothes in.

Just then, Tegwen Rees walks in with baskets of eggs.

"What are you two up to today?" she asks.

"We'll probably go down to see Tom and Anna, and give them a hand with the baskets," Elin says.

"Are the gypsies back already?" their mother asks.

"There'll be enough work for us today, helping them to cut the hazel wands," Gwyndaf says.

"Does your dad need you? Have you asked him?"

"There's not much to do today," says Brython Rees thoughtfully. Clearing the cellar and bringing up the empty barrels to put them on the cart. We'll fetch fresh stock from Jac at the Plough Inn on the way back from the fair on Wednesday. The hay can wait until the end of the week."

With the haymaking season ahead of them, followed by the hustle and bustle of the drovers, Tafarn y Wawr would soon be busy again.

"Oh!" Elin suddenly says. "We saw a company of soldiers on horses going past Pont Goch Cottage last night."

"Dragoons," says Gwyndaf.

"Looking smart, were they?" says Tegwen Rees. "What colour uniforms?"

"Blue," Gwyndaf answers. "And they had enough weapons to start a war."

"We heard their bugle sounding further up the valley," Elin says.

"On the look out for Beca, no doubt," says Brython Rees.

"But there's nothing like that this way," Elin says.

"They're afraid there might be," Gwyndaf says.

"It's us that should be afraid," Tegwen says. "These soldiers aren't here to twiddle their thumbs. Well, there we are – hopefully it'll be a warning to some ..."

"Like who?" Elin asks.

"Oh, you can guarantee that there's some folks ready enough to rabble-rouse and cause trouble," answers her mother.

"What we need now is some common sense," Brython says. "It was almost a battleground in Carmarthen."

"I heard it was a bit of a bloodbath," says Gwyndaf. "Those cavalrymen's swords were slicing in all directions and they didn't care who they slashed. It was only through luck that just one man was badly injured."

"Well, there we are. We don't want to see such a thing over here, do we?" declares his mother.

* * *

Elin and Gwyndaf cross the Sawdde on a wooden footbridge near Pont Goch Cottage. This morning, Edryd Morgan is not in his yard.

They go on further down the valley to Cefn-y-Coed, a field sheltered by thick belts of trees. Across the other side of the field a wooded hillside faces them – Coed yr Arlwydd

Common. After scrambling over trees that have blown down during the winter storms, at last the twins reach a flat clearing. A bender has been erected under the shade of an oak tree and, in front of it, there is a fire licking at a black cooking pot. The cart, without its tarpaulin, stands to one side, loaded with a tidy pile of basket-frames.

"Ah! The future of Tafarn y Wawr!" Mari Lee greets them with a smile.

"Good morning, Mari! It's lovely to see you again!" Elin says. "How has your journeying been since we last saw you? And where is everyone?"

"Same old Elin – questions, questions!" laughs Mari. "We bought a white pony in Llanybydder – but he's got something wrong with one of his hoofs. Jorjo took him first thing down to Llew Lewis' smithy on Carreg Sawdde Common."

"Is Anna Lee around?" Gwyndaf asks.

"She's with her brother, cutting hazel wands."

"We'll give them a hand," Gwyndaf says.

"Not until you've had a taste of the *cawl* I've got going on the fire, you don't," Mari says. "Never pass a full cooking pot."

"We'll come back for that later on," says Gwyndaf.

Tom and Anna are further up the hillside, busy cutting thin wands: the previous year's growth sprouting out of the coppiced hazels.

"What do you want me to do?" Elin asks Tom, once they've greeted each other and caught up on what's been happening since the previous summer.

"You strip the leaves off with the little knife, like you do every year," Tom tells her. "Maybe Gwyndaf could help Anna."

"Oh, I'm sure he will!"

They work hard, and talk just as hard – there isn't a minute's silence.

"We had swords practically shoved up our noses last night," Anna says. She proceeds to tell them the dramatic story.

"Himself – the top brass – thought he'd caught Beca all by himself!" she says, finishing off her tale. "He probably thought he'd get another big medal pinned to his chest and a red feather in his hat. But in the end, it was only a bunch of quiet gypsies and Dicw."

"You weren't laughing like that last night," Tom teases her. "Your knees were knocking like hoofs on a solid road when they caught up to us."

"Oh, poor you, Anna," Elin says. " We saw them passing Pont Goch Cottage. They were just trotting by then, but being confronted by them must have been terrifying."

The conversation goes on, then, to discussing the gypsies' journeys and how they were having to travel along higher and higher routes in the hills, and cross rivers where there were no bridges and sometimes cross fields – all to avoid the toll-gates.

"They're putting barriers and chains across more and more roads now," Tom says. "It's not just the main roads either, but they're charging tolls on the country roads round every town and village."

"And they're the ones full of potholes," Gwyndaf says.

As the conversation meanders on, the pile of wands grows.

"We've got enough now to take them down to Mam so she can start weaving them," Anna says.

"We can go down to the river to cut willow withies after that," Tom says. "Mam likes to edge the baskets with them."

Jorjo hadn't returned from the smithy at Carreg Sawdde Common when they took their load over to the tent. After a bowl of *cawl* each, the youngsters go down to the waterside willows. It is mid-afternoon before those bundles are delivered to Mari Lee.

"They're still not back," she says. "He's not usually this long at the smithy. And it's not that far."

"We've cut enough for today," Tom says. "We'll go down to the common to see what's up."

"Shouldn't we stick to the path beside the river?" Anna asks.

"No, no – we'll be alright walking along the road," Gwyndaf says. "We're on foot, so the toll-keeper at the gate at the bottom of Coed yr Arlwydd hill will open it for us for free."

"We shall be like the royal family!" Elin says.

"Or the Dragoons," Tom adds.

Chapter 3

Dicw the pony has been tethered outside the smithy by the time the four friends arrive at Carreg Sawdde Common. The smithy faces the road from the woods, so it is easy to spot Dicw from afar. But as they get closer they see that the leg with the injured hoof is submerged in a large, deep bucket. The pony's bridle has been tied to the bucket, so he can't lift his leg out of it.

"Forge-water," Tom explains. "There's iron in the water from when the smith cools the metal, and that heals sorts of muscle and skin problems."

"Warts," Gwyndaf says. "I remember coming here with Dad when I was just a little *crwt* to get them treated. They turned black in the end and dropped off!"

"Lovely!" laughs Elin. "What a delightful image!"

"Well – you had them too," her twin retorts, "worse than me, if I remember rightly."

"But where's Tada?" Anna asks.

The top half of the smithy door is open, but it is very dark inside. Tom sticks his head through the gap above the lower half.

"There's no fire in the forge," he says. "Llew Lewis isn't busy at his work, that's why."

Gwyndaf stands beside Tom. Where the fire should be is cold ash and the smell of soot hangs heavy in the air.

Everything looks black. Even the stones of the whitewashed walls have layers of black dust on them. He's about to turn away when he hears the sound of voices getting louder.

"One of those is Tada," Tom says.

"Let's go in, then," says Anna, pushing open the lower half of the door. She walks past the anvil and the big tools in the middle of the floor. At the back of the building, a door leads to the smithy's stable. The voices are coming from there. Anna pushes open the door and sees that her father is standing with his back to her, talking to the blacksmith.

"That's what I heard at Llanybydder fair, Llew. Twm Carnabwth can't put a foot outside his cottage in Pembrokeshire without those constables from London that they've got up in Carmarthen hearing about it. There are spies everywhere. There's a big reward out for information and everyone knows that Twm was the Beca four years ago, when the first toll-gates were smashed up at Efail-wen and Saint Clears."

"So, if Twm Carnabwth isn't Beca this time, who is?" the smith asks. "Oh, is this your little girl, Jorjo? Are my eyes deceiving me, or has she turned into a young maiden already!"

"Come on in, Anna," her father says. "Oh, and you're not alone."

All four come into the smithy stable.

"Are you talking about Beca?" Gwyndaf asks.

"Who isn't?" Llew says. "That's what's on everyone's lips since things started hotting up round here. She was quiet for a while after the first gates were smashed in the west. But since the beginning of the year, Beca's domain has grown."

"She was in Kidwelly in March and in Haverfordwest in April," Gwyndaf says. "I remember the drovers who were staying with us at the inn telling us all about it."

"Beca was in Newcastle Emlyn and Saint Clears at the same time," adds Jorjo. "I heard a farmer at Llanybydder tell of it – each time she had long, loose yellow hair and posh looking women's clothes and was on a white horse."

"But is it the same person every time?" Llew asks.

"Do you think there's more than one in existence?" asks Elin.

"There was only one in Carmarthen, that time that everyone joined together," Anna says.

"And that was in broad daylight," Llew says. "She fears neither the Dragoons nor the Devil."

"D'you know what I think?" Jorjo says. "I think there's one Beca, but she has lots of daughters – and they're all called Beca!"

"And hopefully not one of them will ever be caught!" says Llew. "But you're right, Jorjo – there's one Beca and she's a free spirit. She touches people and fills them with the strength to fight against the injustices of this world."

They all hear the bang of the lower half of the smithy's front door. As they peer through the gloom they can see a dark shadow walking through the workshop and then a burly man of about thirty appears at the stable door. He has flaming red hair and a scar from hot metal under his left ear; even in the half-light of the stable, he's easily recognisable: Dan, Llew Lewis' son.

"Ah-ha, the place is full of people but there's no fire in the forge!" Dan says. "I've just spent three hours at the woollen mill, and the smithy has ground to a halt! Is that your white pony, Jorjo?"

"Yes, he's his," Llew replies. "And there's enough of a fire here in the conversation, for your information. I reckon you could try the pony on that leg now, Jorjo."

The blacksmith stands up and squares his shoulders.

"Could Bob at the mill work the machine, then – after you'd fitted a new wheel for him?"

"Yes, yes," Dan answers. "It's hellish noisy there, but the wool is being spun into yarn perfectly now."

Dan moves over to the bellows beside the forge's big chimney to start blowing air under the coals, and the blacksmith and the gypsy go out to the front to see to the pony. The young people gather in front of Dicw to watch Llew release the bucket and then lift the pony's hoof out of the water. The smith's huge hands can be gentle when needs be, and Dicw seems relaxed with his treatment.

"The badness has come out, I think," Llew says. "And where I had to cut seems to have closed up. Take him for a walk on the common straight away to see how he is. What you need to do now is keep the hoof clean and no heavy work until the fair."

"Will he be alright go do to Llandeilo on Wednesday, d'you think?"

"How far is it? Seven miles from where you are in the woods? Should be alright. But don't load him up too much."

"We'll be walking. And there'll only be empty baskets on

the cart. And we'll have sold the lot before coming back, hopefully."

"Let's see how he is now, then."

Jorjo leads the pony past the end wall of the smithy, towards the common land.

"He's walking pretty well, Tada," Anna notes.

"Yes, and there's no doubt that he's putting his weight on that hoof."

"He's a strong pony too," Gwyndaf says.

"How old is he, Jorjo?" Elin asks.

"Three years old."

Jorjo starts to run, leading the pony along with him. Dicw breaks into a trot, holding his head high. The others join in and before long the sight of them all running along attracts the attention of the other gypsies camped on the common. There are about half a dozen young people and their horses and ponies beside the river. They have led their animals to the river Sawdde to drink, and one or two have ridden their horses into the river. One of the riders in the river gallops over to the white pony.

"Got a new pony, Jorjo?"

"Good morning, Abram. Good to see you again."

"D'you fancy a race, Tom?" Abram challenges.

"No, he's not been too clever. I can't ride him today."

"Some other time, then?" Abram pushes to arrange a future race.

"You've had a good winter," Jorjo says to him. "You've grown as quick as an ash tree – you're almost as tall as our Tom now."

"No, he's on horseback," Tom says. "Easy enough to look big up there!"

Quick as a flash, Abram springs off his horse and stands up straight, shoulder to shoulder with Tom – but there's a broad smile on his face.

"Not bad! Almost up to your shoulder," Abram says. "How old are you now?"

"Eighteen," Tom replies.

"I'll not be long catching up to you, and I'm two years younger than you!"

Abram turns to Gwyndaf. "How old are you, then?"

"Fifteen."

"How about we three have a race?"

"Hey, what about us – Elin and me?" Anna asks. "Girls can run too, you know, Abram."

"Right-o! Five in the race. Better still. Where shall we aim for – what about the toll-gate by the bridge?" Abram is fired-up and itching to compete.

"You can run to the gate with one breath," Jorjo says. "That's not much of a feat. If you're going to have a proper race, race round the common and end at the gate."

"Oo! All right then. Good idea – where shall we start from?"

"Start here, where you're standing now," says Jorjo. "Over to the river. Follow the riverbank and then head straight for Llwyncelyn cottages. Jump over the millrace. Out onto the lane over to Godre'r Garreg farm. Turn back, past the corn mill and Dôl-bant, back to the woollen mill and then a sprint for the gate. That'll show how much puff you've got."

"How far's that?" Elin asks.

"Got to be over a mile, I reckon," says Jorjo.

"Worried now?" Abram asks playfully.

"We'll see," Anna replies.

Jorjo lines them up in a row and asks each to take off their clogs. He says that running is done barefoot.

"No cutting corners, mind you!" Jorjo counts one, two, three and they're off.

Tom bounds ahead on his long legs and Abram keeps so close to him he might as well have been sitting on his shoulder. It's neck and neck between them as they speed along. Very quickly a gap opens up between them and the other three; Gwyndaf is next, a little ahead of Anna and Elin.

"This race is over a mile," Anna says to her friend. "We need to run lightly, not pound the ground like those two bulls."

"But we can't get too far behind them, either!" Elin says.

The two leaders touch the white gate in front of the toll-house beside the bridge. A small man wearing a bowler hat comes to the toll-house door. The two runners turn and aim for the riverbank. After a while, Gwyndaf touches the gate and turns left, following the other two. The small man takes a step outside.

When the two girls arrive at the gate together, they reach out to touch it but get a mouthful from the gatekeeper.

"Don't touch the gate! It's the property of the Trust. Now – on your way!"

The two girls turn to the left without paying much attention to him. But Elin notices the bright eyes of the three small toll-house children, watching the race with great interest.

"The ground's rougher here," Anna says. "Keep your eyes on the ground. Watch you don't trip. There are some big clumps of grass, and rocks here and there. Watch where you put your feet."

Elin keeps her head low and sees that Anna isn't running in a straight line. She's leaning her feet this way and that to avoid obstacles, and springing from one foot to the other with every step.

After leaving the river, there's a stretch on the common and then the millrace. The millrace is fairly wide but the boys have slowed, and are then taking a running jump to clear it.

"We can get across the millrace without slowing and without speeding up," says Anna. "Breathe in on the jump-step!"

And this is how they cross it smoothly. Past the cottages. Keeping to the left, they face a quarter of a mile of rough track across the common to the furthest farm. The two in the lead are already halfway along it, sprinting, and kicking up stones as they gallop and occasionally half-falling as they stumble awkwardly into potholes.

"Come on!" Anna says. "We'll catch up to that brother of yours. His legs are shorter than yours, aren't they. Keep your eyes on where you're going."

"Yes! Let's catch up to Gwyndaf," Elin says.

Elin feels herself lengthening her stride and being suffused with a meditative absorption. She sidesteps a stone and springs from the middle of her foot, transferring energy from its outer edge. Both girls are breathing easily, and Anna is even able to still speak.

"We won't be far behind him by the time we reach Godre'r Garreg."

There is a sharp left-hand turn at the corner before the return journey. Gwyndaf glances at the two girls as he corners, and the look on his face belies his surprise at how close they are. He speeds up.

Tom and Abram pass the cornmill. Their faces are red and showing the strain. Because Abram was challenging him, Tom has run the first half of the race too fast.

Gwyndaf starts to gain on them ...

"Don't let him get too far ahead," Anna says. "Bit of a push ..."

Elin feels her legs respond. Her breathing is still steady. Past Dôl-bant. As he approaches the woollen mill, Tom is holding his side as he runs. Abram passes him but then takes a full-length tumble before straightening back up again. But the gap between Gwyndaf and them is closing, and the girls are keeping pace. They reach the road to the bridge. It's a good hundred yards to the bridge. Gwyndaf overtakes the two older boys on the corner. The race has aroused quite a bit of interest amongst the folk on the common by now and knots of people have gathered along the last hundred yards to cheer on the runners. A huge cheer goes up as the two girls speed past Tom and Abram.

"Right, everything you've got!" Anna yells.

The two accelerate. Fifty yards. Gwyndaf shoots a glance over his shoulder and sees the danger. Head down, he's pounding the air with his fists and hammering the road with his feet. By the slenderest of margins, he touches the white gate first before collapsing in a heap on the common, gasping for breath.

"We almost caught up to you!" Elin says, standing over her brother. "Ten yards more and we would have won!"

"Yes, you and Anna ran fantastically well," Gwyndaf says.

By the gate there is a man on a tall black horse. That isn't a gypsy horse, Elin thinks as she turns to look at him. The man has a black cravat round his throat and he is taking a great deal of interest in the race.

Chapter 4

"Are you coming through the gate or not?" the small toll-keeper asks the man in the black cravat. "It's fourpence for you and your horse."

"I'm looking for the smithy," says the man in the black cravat.

"Well, you've got the Hewl Felen smithy through the gate, over the bridge, through the village and it's on the road to Glansefin. There's another smithy in the village the other side of the parish church and there's another one over the bridge to the south, as you reach Rhyd-y-saint. Which one do you want? The toll is fourpence for a gentleman on a steed, whichever one."

"Llew Lewis' smithy."

"I've never heard of—"

"Excuse me, sir," says Elin, "I couldn't help overhearing. Llew's smithy is over there – over the common towards those houses at Felindre. The end building on the left."

"Thank you, my dear," says the man in the black cravat.

Elin looks him in the face for the first time. She sees a narrow face with high, prominent cheekbones. He has curly, salt-and-pepper side-whiskers. A square jaw and a set, determined mouth. But it is his eyes that hold her attention – they are hawk-like in their intensity, glittering, and they don't miss a thing.

"And you two girls ran a really good race." The man in the black cravat looks at the three boys, who are still lying on the ground, panting and gasping. "It wouldn't surprise me if you could still run round the common the other way!"

He receives an appreciative smile from Elin and Anna and then rides off in the direction of the smithy.

"For goodness' sake, thanks for nothing, girls!" The toll-keeper is not happy. "I've lost another fourpence now that could have gone towards feeding these here children of mine."

He turns on his heel and goes back in through the open door of the toll-house.

"Wasn't the end of that race was something!" Jorjo has walked over to them by now. "You held your ground, Gwyndaf, fair play to you, but you were within a hair's breadth of catching up to him, girls. And as for the two wild horses, well you should take account of the length of the race before turning the tap full on, shouldn't you?"

"At least I wasn't last to reach the gate!" Tom says, punching Abram playfully.

"Dicw's hoof seems to be holding up, Tada," says Anna.

"Yes. We'd better be getting back to the Coed. There's work to be done on the baskets. Are you two coming?"

Tom gets up, ready to follow his father.

"I've got nothing that particularly needs doing," Gwyndaf says. "I'll come with you if you could do with a bit more help."

He stands at Anna's side.

"Elin," he says to his sister, "Dad took two taps for barrels to Llew Lewis a few weeks ago. He'll be needing them now.

Could you go and ask for them? Will you be alright to go home over the bridge after?"

It wasn't even a mile to the Tafarn y Wawr but Elin smiled as she saw how her brother had succeeded in getting Anna to himself.

"I'll go to the smithy now," she says, and that doesn't bother her either.

Dan is tending the fire in the workshop when Elin walks up to the open door. She watches him turn the iron in the coals, which are glowing red by now, staring into the depths of the heat as the metal turns from black to red, and from red to white. Dan straightens up suddenly and steps quickly to the anvil to strike the hot metal with a series of carefully-aimed blows until it folds slowly over to form a curl at the end of a metal pole. After more scrutiny and further blows, it is plain that he is pleased with the result. He plunges the hot metal into a trough, causing the water to hiss and belch clouds of steam.

He is known as Dan Dowlais in the village, and this is what runs through Elin's head. He had left the smithy as a sixteen-year-old youth. Although he had learned the trade of blacksmithing from his father, he'd gone to the Merthyr area to make his fortune in the ironworks. He worked loading the furnaces in Dowlais, but he wasn't there more than two years. Despite the money being better in Merthyr, things were not good there. He left pretty quickly after what had come to be known as the Merthyr Rising, when the workers took over the town until the army arrived. Although he'd been back at the smithy for twelve years, in the village he would forever be Dan Dowlais.

Dan raises his head and notices Elin standing in the doorway.

"Another curl for the vicar's gate," he says to her. "They're having new gates for that big house of theirs in the village. That's what the church tithes are spent on, you see! But at least a few pennies roll through the door of this smithy."

"Dad's asking for his barrel taps, Dan."

"What taps?"

"Gwyndaf and I brought them down to the smithy three weeks back, maybe a month."

"Did you give them to me?"

"No, to Llew."

"Uhh! And what's he done with them, then? He forgets about these jobs until he trips over them ... Two taps for the pub, you say?"

Dan searches round the smithy.

"No sign of them. I'd better go and have a word with him ..."

He turns to go out to the stable, but Elin stops him.

"No, don't. He's got someone with him. I saw the horse outside. Your dad was standing in the corner over there when we gave him the taps ..."

"By here? ... Oh, what do we have here on this block of wood?"

He holds up two metal items.

"Yes, that's them, Dan."

"What's the matter with them?"

Dan stands by the smithy door, studying the taps he is holding.

"The end you hit has cracked on both of them. You see this curved bit in front of where the tap opens? That's the part Dad hits with a mallet to wedge the tap into a new barrel. But these two have cracked round the tap and they leak beer, even when the tap itself is closed."

"Goodness, we don't want to be wasting good beer. Well, it's clear that Dad hasn't tripped over these taps yet ..."

"Any chance of having them to take home to him tonight?"

"Tonight! I've got—"

"But they've been here for weeks, Dan! And it's Llandeilo fair on Wednesday – some people travel a long way for it and they want a drop of beer from us when they pass in the dawn light."

"Oh yes, and want another drop on the way home, probably. Well, alright, *croten*. I won't be long fixing these cracks. Sit yourself down if you can find somewhere."

Dan carries the taps to the fire.

Elin looks about her. There is a wooden chair beside the back door of the stable. She goes over to sit on it.

She watches Dan concentrating on his work. She glances round at the amazing equipment filling the smithy. Then she hears voices behind her. She recognises the sound of the blacksmith's, and the other voice must belong to the stranger: the man in the black cravat. She turns her head and picks up fragments of sentences. She isn't being nosy, so much as wanting to find out more about the man in the black cravat.

She's never seen him in the village before. No, she tells herself, she's not eavesdropping on the private conversation in the stable but when she suddenly hears the word 'Rebecca' she pricks up her ears.

Yes, there it is again. The voice of the stranger.

"... a new Rebecca ... everyone knows about Twm ..."

Then she hears some of what the blacksmith is saying.

"... things are bitter now ... this isn't play-acting any more ... the swords are drawn ..."

Then the voice of the man in the black cravat comes again.

"... that's why we need to shift the pressure from the west ... her in the Tywi valley ... but it must be kept quiet ... ears and tongues are wagging ... very dangerous ..."

Then the blacksmith again, who has obviously stood up and is pacing about the stable. He comes closer to the door. Elin hears the sound of a metal chain being shaken but the smith's next sentence is totally clear.

"We need a chain like this iron chain here. Every link in the chain is safe but any one link only touches two others – the one in front of it and the one behind. This link doesn't know how long the chain is, nor who's at the far end of it – but it knows the chain is strong. That's the way forward. Keep the line of communication secret and move the message carefully from link to link down the chain before mustering the Daughters."

The voice of the stranger answers then, but he is at the far side of the room and Elin can't hear a word of what he says.

"There we go," says Dan, from beside the forge, "the two

taps are watertight now. They shouldn't leak even one drop of your father's beer. Maybe he'll save enough to give me a pint! I just need to cool them off ..."

The sound of the water hissing again. But Elin hears the blacksmith's final words.

"Right, I'm off to see Jac Griffiths at the Plough Inn. It's time for us to start winning some battles. Having a smashing time while smashing gates is no good at all if we lose the day. We need to win the day once in a while. It's time we started winning again!"

"Here you are!" Dan Dowlais hands her the taps. "They're still quite warm. Leave them in the water for a while for them to cool more, so I can get back to this gate for the vicar."

By the time Elin leaves the smithy, the man in the black cravat and the blacksmith have left the stable through the far door. They are standing beside the black horse. The stranger nods towards Elin.

"This one runs like a filly, Llew."

"Does she now?" Elin feels as if the blacksmith is suddenly paying her a lot more attention.

"And the dark-skinned girl who was with her ..."

"I saw her this afternoon. Anna. Jorjo the gypsy's daughter. Well, running creates a chain, doesn't it?"

The two men exchange a look.

Elin takes her leave of the smithy. As she goes past the white gate at Pont Carreg Sawdde, she sees the small man in the bowler hat again. He frowns at her.

"Two feet. No good to me. Not one penny to pass," he says sourly.

Two barefoot children run out of the toll-house; they look thin and sallow. Although they're bashful, they can't help looking at Elin in amazement.

She reaches the turnpike road, crosses it and starts to follow the footpath up through the fields, past Cae-rhyn, towards Tafarn y Wawr. There is no one else on the path. She starts running lightly. She tries to remember Anna's instructions. Don't push yourself too hard too early. Keep your eyes on the obstacles on the ground. Jink round them. Spring back from the sides of your feet. Feel nimble and light on your feet. Her steps speed up, even though the path rises steeply ...

Chapter 5

Although it is still early morning, the crowds on Rhosmaen Street are too dense for a horse and cart to travel through Llandeilo. It is fair day, and many people have risen early to travel to the town. As they have business in the fair, Elin and Gwyndaf arrive in town in the cart with their father as stalls are being erected along the streets and in the churchyard, having left Tegwen Rees in charge at Tafarn y Wawr. The stallholders fight for space amongst the pig-carts and cattle on sale. Other people arrive, mounted on fine horses, carving out a path through the middle of the crowd.

Brython Rees guides his mare along Crescent Road to the rear of the White Horse Inn, where he unhitches her from the cart. Gwyndaf goes off to stable the mare. Brython is meeting two drovers for breakfast in the King's Head, and after that he needs to go to the Bank of the Black Ox. But before jumping down from the cart, he pulls a pale blue ribbon out of his waistcoat pocket.

"Would you like to wear this in your hair today, Elin, seeing as it's fair day?" Brython asks.

"Thanks, Dad," Elin says. "It's very pretty. Where did you get it, so early in the day?"

"It used to belong to my sister," her father says. "Gwladys. She died young. Haven't I told you about her before?"

"No, I don't think so."

"Wear it. Keep it. It goes with the colour of your eyes."

Elin ties the ribbon in her hair. Then she smiles at her father and puts her basket over her arm, ready to go off to do the shopping her mother needs.

"I'll be going to the warehouse at the top of Bridge Street after," Brython says. "There's a chest of tea to be collected for the shop in the village. One of the lads there can fetch it out on a trolley and we'll put it in the cart, in the back there."

As he has a sizeable cart to carry barrels, from time to time Brython Rees gets quite a bit of business carrying goods for other businesses in the area. He can also carry travellers, if needs be.

Elin goes to King Street to make a start. This is where the shop selling flour is. She has an order for enough sacks of flour to last the pub a month. This was her favourite port of call, because she didn't have to carry anything – the shopkeeper would send the sacks to the pub before the end of the week.

"How much did you say the price is this month?" She stares at the youth behind the counter as if he has horns growing out of his head. "That's more than a quarter again than what it was last month."

"That's what's down on this chit," the lad replies, flustered.

"But we place and order every month and pay every month!"

"That's the best price I can offer you."

"Well, then you ask your Mr Harries if he can give me a better price. We'll never make a profit like this – the price is too high. Everyone has to make a living!"

"Is there a problem, my dear?" Watcyn Harries, the proprietor, has come over to the counter on hearing raised voices. After hearing Elin's protestations, he shakes his head in sympathy.

"It breaks my heart, Elin *fach*. You're good customers, but the cost to us – well, it's gone through the roof. There's a shortage of wheat and barley, you see – wet summers and poor harvests last year and the year before, and on top of that the parliament in London are refusing permission for any to come in from other countries overseas. Imports would bring down the price for ordinary folk like us. But no, that would mean less profit for the landlords, you see. They look after their own by passing the Corn Laws. And on top of that, carting a load of flour to Tafarn y Wawr means paying the tolls at all these gates. And the tolls have risen half as much again over the last few years. Rhosmaen Gate, Maenordeilo Gate, Pont ar Dywi Gate, Glan Sawdde Gate – that's four gates for you in seven miles! Sixpence a time for a horse and cart! Two shillings, Elin *fach*. A fortnight's wages for a farm worker! Oh, I'm really sorry but I can't sell the flour at a loss and that's the lowest I can offer you, one of my valued customers, for this month. We can only hope things look up, Elin *fach*."

"We try to support businesses in our local market town," Elin says, feeling her colour rising, "but these prices are scandalous!"

"If you go further afield to buy, you'd just have to pay more in tolls to cart everything home through the toll-gates,"

Watcyn Harries replies, before moving down the counter to another customer complaining about the price increases.

It was the same story in every shop and at every stall. Everyone's costs are higher, so all the prices had gone up. Elin fills her basket, but her purse is pretty empty. She sees Anna standing with the cartful of baskets in front of the Shire Hall on Carmarthen Street. Surprise, surprise, Gwyndaf is there too. Elin looks at the huge load of baskets.

"Things haven't started to sell yet, have they?"

"It doesn't look too good today," Anna replies

"Strong baskets! Baskets for a farm task, baskets for a home task! What's the price? – just ask!" Jorjo is advertising his wares by shouting across the street. Mari Lee, standing beside him, proffers a basket to a passing couple but they look down and shake their heads.

"Come now," Mari says, "you can't leave Llandeilo fair without one of the best baskets in the county!"

"Oh, what's amiss with this fair, I wonder?" Elin says, with frustration in her voice. "It's as if there's a black cloud hanging over everyone and everything."

"Well, here's someone with a feather in his cap," Anna says.

All three young people turn their attention towards a straight-backed man in military uniform, with a tricorn hat on his head and a sword hanging from his belt. He is more decorated than an ordinary soldier. He walks with a bearing that shows he is important. Two infantrymen, armed with guns, follow him.

"He's come here from Carmarthen," says Gwyndaf.

"Colonel Love, someone who saw him arrive at the Cawdor Hotel told me. He's the head of all the soldiers in the three counties here. By God, there's more here than he had against Napoleon!"

"There's a certain softness to his eyes," says Mari Lee, hearing their conversation. "Maybe he has a heart underneath all that braid."

"Why's he in Llandeilo today, then?" Elin asks.

"There's a meeting of bigwigs in the hall, that's what I heard," Gwyndaf says. "Rice-Trevor, Lord Dynevor will be there."

"But doesn't he live in London?" asks Elin.

"The city of very, very large rats," says Mari Lee.

"He's back here to uphold law and order," Gwyndaf explains.

Over the next five minutes, the little knot of people standing beside the cartful of baskets see the chief officials of the town and the county arrive and disappear into the entrance to the hall. They see the town's magistrates; the lord of the big house and his chief officials; parish clerks; the master of the workhouse at Ffair-fach, just over the bridge; and several constables sent from London.

"What I'd like to know," Elin says to her brother, "is how come you recognise all these important people?"

"A good question, Elin," says Anna, joining in with the leg-pulling. "They say that these big people have little people to carry tales to them, isn't that so?"

"Speaking a bit of sense in the fair – instead of gossiping, as others like to do!" Gwyndaf retorts. "That, and reading the *Carmarthen Journal*."

Elin notices a young man suddenly turn to look at them. He has a pencil and notebook in his hand. As he catches her eye, he nods to her. He turns and jots something else in his notebook, closes it, and walks over to them.

"How's the fair shaping up for you today? Do you have an opinion on the big questions of the day?"

"Strong baskets! Baskets for a farm task, baskets for a home task! What's the price? – just ask!" calls Jorjo.

"Everyone's shaking their heads today," Elin says. "Selling's hard, and so is paying. Is that the sort of thing you're collecting in your little book?"

"Dylan Lloyd," he says. "I work on the local newspaper called—"

"The *Journal*!" Gwyndaf says. "I read your articles every week. We take the paper in our pub, you see."

"And which pub is that?"

"You aren't half fond of asking questions, aren't you?" says Elin, a little smile playing on her lips.

"That's my job," Dylan answers. "Unearthing buried things that some people would prefer stayed that way."

Gwyndaf explains who they are and then the pair of them start discussing the meeting that has been arranged for that morning in the Shire Hall.

"There was a similar meeting in Newcastle Emlyn on Friday," Dylan says. "They're calling for a local constabulary to be formed and the town magistrates are appealing for more soldiers."

"Men in show-off hats," Mari Lee comments.

"Not that that seems to be working particularly well," Dylan says. "The Dragoons were sent from Carmarthen on Monday night, some to Newcastle Emlyn and some to Saint Clears – but all the while Beca was in Fishguard and the gate there was smashed to smithereens. The Dragoons returned from Newcastle to Carmarthen without seeing a thing. And then at four o'clock in the morning yesterday, hundreds of the Daughters of Rebecca destroyed the gate at Llanegwad."

"But Llanegwad's not far from Llandeilo!" Elin exclaims. "Just down the road, on the way to Nantgaredig."

"This one was pretty vicious – the Daughters pulled the roof off the toll-house this time, as well as firing guns in the air. More and more of them are carrying guns now."

"That's no surprise, with the number of soldiers about," Gwyndaf says.

"And there's more on the way," Dylan says. "You see that big chap in the black coat beside the entrance to the hall? He's a newspaperman from London. Thomas Foster; he writes for *The Times*, the most important of the London papers."

"Got his nose in the air, then," Mari Lee says.

"Got his nose to the scent, more like," says Dylan. "He noses out facts that the big nobs would rather didn't see the light of day. He's already had one brilliant article published about what's happening here – and enumerated eleven toll-gates on the journey from Pontarddulais to Carmarthen alone. He's said that there's not a three-mile stretch of road in Carmarthenshire without a gate or a barrier or a chain that you have to pay to have opened."

"He understands how things are, then," Gwyndaf says.

"He talks to people on the street, you see. Some of the papers see only disorder and destruction, but he sees that there's a reason fuelling the actions. I'll have to join him now – the meeting will be starting shortly. If anyone there speaks Welsh, it's me who translates for him and explains what's being referred to."

At that, Dylan Lloyd crosses the street and, after the two journalists exchange a few words, Elin and Gwyndaf see them disappear into the grand entrance of the Shire Hall.

"I don't have much faith in things changing after this meeting," says Gwyndaf.

"But at least maybe we'll get the truth in some of the papers," Elin says. "Hey, what's the time?"

"Ten to twelve, according to the clock on the hall."

"There's a theatre group from Crymych performing skits in the yard at the back of the White Horse at midday," Elin says. "Anyone coming?"

"Can I go and see the skits with them, Dad?" Anna asks.

"Well, we don't need any help here," Jorjo answers.

"Only the help of the horseshoe, which brings a bit of luck," Mari Lee says.

The three friends make their way to the back of the White Horse. There is already a sizeable crowd, along with a wagon in a corner of the yard with nothing on it save for a harp. Next to the wagon is a tent, its door opening onto the stage. This is where the actors will prepare themselves and change costumes during the performance.

Tom Lee comes over to join them. He has been working in the stables, taking charge of farmers' horses and looking after them.

"They're not tipping much today," he says.

The crowd's spirit rises as a jesting performer arrives onstage, dressed colourfully, beating a hand drum and spouting verses, indicating that the show is about to begin. He declares that this is a service of thanksgiving for four beloved characters in Carmarthenshire these days: Vicar Blubbery Bevan; the Chief Food Taster of the Workhouse; Bish the Bullock, the steward of the Dinefwr estate; and Tomi Toll-gate, collector of pennies for the Turnpike Trust. As he names the characters in turn, a fierce but good natured 'Boo!' rises from the audience.

From scene to scene, each character in turn comes on stage to receive thanks for the huge favours each is doing for the country folk and society in general. The crowd laughs at everything and joins in with the satirical songs – but a sharp undercurrent under all the fun cuts to the root of every injustice that is palpable in Llandeilo fair that day.

In the middle of Bish the Bullock's scene, when the performers thank the steward of the estate for raising rents and throwing people off their farms if they have money troubles, Elin notices a large, hunched man in a brown suit and matching bowler hat turn angrily away from the stage and push his way through the crowd, making for the entrance to go out into the street. Some start to push back, until he raises his stick to part the crowd.

"Who's that sourpuss with the little moustache?" Elin asks.

"It's Bishop, the chief steward of Newton House in Dinefwr Park," says her brother.

"Need a piss, Bish?" someone shouts.

Bishop stops and turns towards the shout, but the heckler has hidden himself in the crowd.

"Yes, you can see he's got big slack cheeks like a bullock, hasn't he?" says Elin.

As she follows the steward's journey towards the entrance, Elin sees that the man in the black cravat is standing at the back of the crowd.

At the end of the performance, after paying their pennies and shouting for another song, Brython Rees comes over to the four young people.

"We need to fetch the barrels from the Plough at two o'clock, so I'll see you back in this yard about half an hour before that."

When Elin looks again towards the back of the crowd, the man in the black cravat is no longer there.

Chapter 6

The Plough Inn is at Rhosmaen, located on the turnpike road about a mile outside Llandeilo. On fair days, the place is full of travellers from first light until evening. Farmers, local craftspeople and a sprinkling of drovers are the usual customers. Jac Griffiths, the innkeeper, is known for his good beer. The brewery is housed in outbuildings behind the inn and there Jac, his wife, Leisa, and Ann, their daughter, boil up the wort, which is left to ferment, and then casked. However, on fair days, kitchen and bar work are more important – seeing to customers' needs.

Jac is a short, stocky man with arms muscled by constantly lifting full 18-gallon casks. He walks round the tables in his leather apron, giving the occasional friendly punch to someone's arm, exchanging a few words with another. Every now and again something sets him off laughing and he roars with his head tipped back and his mouth wide open.

Elin has been there to collect casks of beer with her father before, but never before on a fair day. As she tails her father between the tables, she is amazed at how packed the place is.

"Hey, Jac, the beer's gone up again!" one of his customers shouts at the innkeeper.

"I want to be a rich man, like you, that's why," Jac replies.

"Yeah, it's only laughing water, after all," says another drinker, looking mournfully into his tankard.

"Well, it's not doing its work on the one who's drinking it yet!" Jac booms, throwing his head back and laughing heartily again. "Ann, fetch that jug over here for a top up, he's making short work of this one."

"Bring us some, over here, after," says a young man sitting at another table. "We've come a long way – we've heard about the good quality of the beer at the Plough."

"Where are you from, if I may be so bold as to ask?" Jac enquires. "I haven't seen either of you here before."

"This is Eban, my mate, and I'm Wil – William Williams. I'm a farmer's son from Ffos-yr-efel in Pontarddulais and this is my neighbour.

"Come over for the fair, have you?"

"Of course, to see which way the wind's blowing."

"And was there a gentle breeze today, then?"

"No. There was a fierce wind. From the west."

Jac hesitates for half a second, then nods as if they understand each other.

"Ann, fetch that jug over to Wil and his mate here." Jac stoops over the table and, in a voice a shade lower than the hubbub of the inn: "Out the back, in the brewhouse in five minutes?"

Wil raises his tankard and hides his quiet smile in his pint pot.

Jac turns his attention to the Tafarn y Wawr table.

"Good to see you, Brython. And the twins. And isn't this young lady with the ribbon a picture! They both look as if they're not afraid of hard work, either of them. Are they a help to you and Tegwen with all the work in the pub?"

"They're coming along," says Brython, "but it's hard work."

"True enough. Ann, when you've finished flirting with the strangers at that table over there, bring a glass over to this table. We'll load the casks into the cart after."

Jac moves on to the next table.

Who should walk into the Plough Inn just then, but the man in the black cravat. Elin sees him quickly scan from table to table and then, without drawing attention to himself, walk over to the table where Llew Lewis the blacksmith is sitting. He leans over to say something in his ear, then continues towards Jac. He does the same with him, then exits through the side door of the inn. Shortly after, Llew drains his glass and stands up to take his leave.

"Back to the smithy, my friends," he says as he passes the Tafarn y Wawr family. "See you again soon, hopefully. We'll have to drop by to sample the new beer, Brython."

The smith leaves via the front door.

"We'd better go and load up," says their father to the twins. "Let's go."

Behind the inn, the horse is still hitched up to the cart.

"Go and see if anyone's about, Elin, and we'll take the cart up to the double doors."

Elin walks up to the door of the brewhouse and she can hear voices inside. She knocks on the door, and opens it when Jac calls to her.

"Ah, Elin," Jac says, "the casks are by the double doors above the cellar, in the room through there. I'll be with you now."

Elin goes through and opens the double doors to let her father and brother in.

"Did he say which casks are for us?" Brython asks.

Just then, Jac and Wil Ffos-yr-efel come over.

"Three hogsheads is what you wanted today, that's what you said, didn't you, Brython?"

When Brython nods, Jac turns to his companion. "Wil here has come all the way from Pontarddulais to give a helping hand in getting the casks into the cart, Brython!"

The four men lift the heavy casks into the back of the cart in no time; they are careful to keep them upright.

"The beer in these has been cleared of dregs for you, Brython," says the brewer. "They've been standing in the cellar for a fortnight and they're ready to drink tonight, if you want."

"But the sediment will get stirred up and cloud the beer on the journey home," Brython says. "I'd rather let them settle for a couple of days."

"Take my advice, Brython, you'll be needing them tonight. I decanted the beer into these fresh casks last night and there's not much sediment in there now. They've just been brought up from the cellar so they're nice and sparkling and cold. Tap them high for tonight – the top halves will be perfect."

"How do you know I'm going to be so busy tonight?"

"There's a meeting in your pub tonight, late on, Brython. You'll need these two ready to serve to the table ..."

"But no one's asked me ..."

"Sometimes you have to tell, not ask. And no one refuses

if Beca says – just you remember that, Brython."

"Beca?"

"You've twigged it, mate. Some fat farmer from Saint Clears said 'No' to Beca, and before morning his cattle were in his wheat fields. Don't refuse, Brython."

Jac turns back to Wil.

"You'd better go now, Wil. Go back to the pubs in town. Don't drink more than you have to – just enough to be sociable. Iori'll be in the Castle for six. Another friend will tell those he trusts. You do the same. Here, nine o'clock tonight. Everyone that can is to bring clothes and weapons. I've organised horns. The blue coats go out at eight. Remember, time is of the essence. Off you go now. And don't draw attention to yourself."

Wil nods to the Tafarn y Wawr family, and departs.

"What the hell has got into you, Jac?" Brython asks in an earnest voice.

"We have to keep the pressure up, *bois*. The west is crawling with soldiers and Dragoons at the moment. They're like a plague of locusts across the land. We, in this valley, have to play our part now. Wil is taking the same message to Pontarddulais ..."

"Good God. This isn't playing our part, Jac, this is playing with fire." Brython sounds deeply distressed. "The Dragoons are patrolling in Llandeilo and Llangadog too."

"Not tonight. Our Iori is a stable lad at the King's Head and the Dragoons call in there frequently. He finds out their plans. He gets a message down to me. They're leaving Llandeilo at eight tonight to go over to Pumsaint."

"Pumsaint? That's a twenty-six-mile round trip. They'll be at it all night."

"That's our chance. We're getting a gang together to leave at nine."

"Which gate?"

"We'll have decided by then. There's plenty of choice! It'll be another gang that'll be with you ..."

"Llangadog? But ..."

"Two Becas in the valley on the same night. Their heads'll be spinning."

"My head's spinning now," Brython says, sitting down on an empty cask in the courtyard. "Oh, I don't know what Tegwen's going to say to this, I really don't."

"Tonight is easy. We've been able to see a lot of people that we need to because of the fair. And this will be the first time Beca has struck over here. But we'll be keeping in touch in a different way after tonight. We need a chain."

"A chain?"

The words she'd heard in the smithy at Carreg Sawdde Common come back to Elin.

"A role for the quickest among us," Jac says, glancing at the twins. "Llew the blacksmith will explain tonight. None of you knows anyone further than Llew in the line of messages. Do you understand?"

The jolly host demeanour of the innkeeper has disappeared by now, replaced by a look of determination and fervour.

"Remember – sharing information puts other people in danger. I know I can depend on you, Brython. And on you two youngsters. And this isn't a game. This is something we have to change. And we have to do it properly. Things have to change."

Jac steps into the middle of the yard and shouts so there is no doubt for anyone who happens to be within earshot what is being discussed in the brewery's doorway.

"There we go, then, a load of the best beer in the west! Llangadog will feel better after a swig of this! Safe journey to you, now!"

Jac turns on his heel and heads back into the inn.

Not much is said in the cart on the way home.

"Did you two know anything of these plans?" Brython asks the twins.

"I'd heard nothing until just now," Gwyndaf answers.

"No ..." says Elin, unable to look at her father.

By the time they reach the ford at Rhyd-y-Saeson, Llew Lewis' cart is waiting for them.

"Thought it would be best if we cross the Tywi together, in case a cask tips into the river," says the blacksmith. "I could jump in after it!"

There was no danger of that happening. The river level is low this summer and the cart makes it across the shingle of the ford with no trouble. They get up onto the bank on the far side and then travel along a straight, fairly new road towards Ynys-y-moch. By leaving the turnpike road and going across the ford, the two men avoid paying one toll at Pont ar Dywi on the turn-off for Llangadog and another toll at the toll-gate beside Glan Sawdde farmhouse. The blacksmith would still have to pay a toll to cross Pont Carreg Sawdde to reach his smithy.

But there would be no avoiding the next gate: the gate to get from the Rhyd-y-Saeson road onto Carreg Sawdde Common.

"Sixpence for a horse and cart," says the gatekeeper to Llew Lewis.

"It's daylight robbery, not a toll," the blacksmith says. "I refuse to pay."

"If that's the way you want to play it, your name will go down in the big book I keep on my desk in the house," says the toll-keeper. "Then you'll be up in front of the magistrates. You'll get a two pound fine – plus costs. So, what'll it be, sixpence now or two pounds or more later?"

"There's another choice," Llew replies. "Not to pay at all. You open the gate, put my name in the book and to hell with you."

"Your loss," the gatekeeper says. "You'll end up in the workhouse if you go on like that."

When the Tafarn y Wawr cart moves up to the gate, he shouts: "Sixpence for the horse and cart, Brython Rees."

The publican places a sixpence in his hand without looking at him or saying a word.

When their ways part for the smithy and the pub, Elin asks her father: "Why didn't we refuse to pay, like Llew did, Dad?"

"Good grief, *croten*. Where's your common sense? You can't just challenge the authorities openly, in broad daylight! They have the power to erect the gates and they have the law behind them to demand payment somehow or another. They have the power and the pounds; it is we who give and keep on giving."

"That's how it is in broad daylight, Dad," Gwyndaf says. "Maybe it'll be different when night falls."

Chapter 7

"Fetch that jug over here, my dear, when you get a chance, Elin *fach*!"

The tables in Tafarn y Wawr had filled up early that evening. Down in the cellar, Brython has had to tap one of the new casks, exactly as Jac at the Plough had predicted. Thankfully, the beer had run clear, and everyone seems satisfied.

Despite that, the conversations passing back and forth are anything but satisfied. Apart from Elin and Tegwen Rees, there are only men present. These farmers and craftsmen are complaining that everything they had bought had never been dearer, and the prices of everything they had to sell had fallen.

There are a number of farmhands present too. Their wages haven't risen for years – but in this matter they sympathise with the farmers who employ them.

"I went on my pony to Llandeilo fair this morning. I went all the way round through Capel Gwynfe and over the hills to avoid the toll-gates – but blow me, the Trust had only gone and put up barriers here and there, just because of the fair! Fourpence every time!"

"Yes, John, you're right. And the Trust says it's raising tolls and using the money to improve the state of the roads. But it's us, we who live in each parish, who look after these small country roads – the money they're collecting gets spent elsewhere."

"Yes, indeed – the money ends up in the very deep pockets of the very high-ups."

"You're right, it's for pockets and not potholes!"

In every part of the country Turnpike Trusts have been formed by Act of Parliament, each with a moneyed board of trustees, to raise tolls on road users. The money raised is supposed to be used for road improvements.

"You can't trust the trustees – that's the plain, honest truth of it."

"The world's changing, you know – you have to get stuff to market quicker these days."

"Oh, I don't know about that," Brython Rees says, joining in with his customers' conversation. "This pub's on a drovers' route – they're still operating as they always have. They're free on the mountains – you can go from here to England without paying a penny!"

"Yes, but how much longer will that go on, Brython? There are gates as you go up onto the Black Mountain now. There's a gate on Hewl y Gelli, a gate by Pont Clydach and one at Cwm Llwyd."

"They're trying to catch the carts carrying coal from Brynaman and limestone from the quarries at Pant-y-ffynnon, they are – they know we have to have the goods and they milk us."

"There was no toll on carts carrying lime years ago – and that's how it should always be. We're paying to improve land we rent off the big landowner, and his Trust is making us pay tolls for doing it!"

"But the drovers are fortunate enough to be left alone,"

says the publican. "That's how it's been for centuries, and that's how it'll be again."

"You can't be too sure, Brython! Have you heard about the railways and the steam engines? They've got them in the ironworks and coal mines in the Valleys ..."

"Those are little lines in the works, mate. We're talking about the travelling public."

"Hold on a minute. The big trains have reached Bristol already – what's to say they won't reach us here before long? The English have no need of drovers England since they arrived."

"He's talking nonsense," Brython says. "The train line has stopped at Bristol because it's reached the sea – the train can't float over the waves, can it?"

"*Bois bach*, we're getting off the subject, rather," says Llew the blacksmith. "Let's get back to the gates and the toll-houses and what we can do in the Sawdde valley tonight."

"Well, the drovers will be here as long as I am, I'm sure of that," the publican replies. "For goodness' sake, where would the old Duke of Wellington have been without Welsh beef to feed his troops with before Waterloo?"

"Yes, but the old Duke went into the government in London afterwards, didn't he? And pretty quickly forgot about little things like that as soon as he was there."

"He forgot about the furnaces of Merthyr once the war was over," Dan Dowlais says. "There was a good price paid for Welsh iron when he wanted canons, but they gave us nothing afterwards. And there was no one to plead our case in London, was there?"

"No need to bring politics into this, Dan," says a moon-faced man whose land is in the lowlands of the Tywi valley. "Getting rid of the toll-gates and keeping a couple of pence in our own pockets, that's what we want."

"Yeah – hear, hear!"

"It's not polling we want, but pulling down!"

"But you can't avoid the fact that politics is at the root of the problem, mate!" Dan is on his feet now. "How many of you in this room has the vote? Two or three, maybe? We have no voice, and so no one takes any notice of our problems."

"The hope is, friends ..." One of the deacons from the Baptist chapel is on his feet now. He gives a little cough before continuing in a measured manner. "The hope is that these protests will draw to the attention of the authorities the great injustices in the way that the ordinary people of Wales are treated. Thereafter, the hope is that the good people in whose hands the power lies will pass laws to change things to alleviate our tribulations somewhat."

"Good people?" Dan Dowlais raises his voice. "What world are you living in, man? It's bad people who are in power. Privileged and wealthy people. There'll be no good until they're got rid of and then we'll have a better state of affairs."

"And how do you propose getting rid of them, my friend?"

"They hang our folks!" cries Dan. "Shooting one or two of them would be no bad thing!"

That causes a bit of a stir in the room. Llew jumps to his feet and tries to reason with his son.

"There'll be no talk like that in this part of the world!"

"But some of the Daughters of Rebecca carry guns," Dan says.

"To draw attention, not to take life," his father retorts.

"Maybe the guns need aiming at better targets – there are bad people in our midst."

"That's enough, Dan! Not another word!"

But Dan's face is as red as his hair by now, and he has completely lost his temper.

"I'm telling you, the big men that keep us on the leash understand nothing but violence ..."

"Out!"

Dan falls silent and turns to face the blacksmith.

"Get out!"

Moments of heavy silence pass. Then Dan turns and walks out through the pub door.

"We can deal with our own problems in our own way," the smith says quietly as he closes the door. "That's the way of Beca, isn't it?"

"There's more sense to be had in this mallet than in the heads of some of those blockheads upstairs," Tegwen Rees says to her husband when they are both down in the cellar.

"It's all topsy-turvy," agrees Brython. "Everyone gets to say what they like. Everyone airing their own grievances."

"We must make sure we stay out of this, Brython," his wife warns. "It's not good for business."

"We can't cross them, though, Tegwen. We're part of the community here. These people are our customers."

"But drovers are our main customers. And they don't start mud-slinging."

"They've chosen the hard option." Gwyndaf has come downstairs with an empty jug by now, and joins the discussion. "Fog and rain and mountain bogs are the way of the drover, because they have to avoid the roads along the valleys."

"That's how it's been for centuries," Brython says. "The moorland and upland passes were the only way to travel before the lowlands were drained, and bridges built."

"You're not going with them tonight, are you, Brython? You'll end up in Carmarthen Gaol! And we'll be in the workhouse."

"I'll go on behalf of the family, if you like," Gwyndaf says. "There'll be enough of a crowd, and no one will recognise us, and the Dragoons are in Pumsaint and—"

"No, you are not going! You're too young!" Tegwen says.

"I was born first. Am I old enough to go then, Mam?" Elin comes down the stairs.

"You're a girl, Elin, and there's no place for our daughter in such a thing! How could you represent the family? Leave it to the men."

"No daughters in the Daughters of Rebecca, Mam?"

"Beer! The throats round the tables are drying out and we're having trouble getting the words out!" one of the customers shouts down the cellar stairs.

Tegwen Rees hurries up the stairs with two full jugs of beer. As she goes through the door at the top of the stairs into the main room she is wearing a smile.

By now the blacksmith is on his feet, explaining the night's plan.

"We're meeting at midnight at the Rhyd-y-saint crossroads. You can get there from several different directions without encountering a single gate. Everyone will have soot on their faces. Wear whatever women's clothes are in your family, especially a bonnet or something on your head. We don't want anyone to be recognised. If you can get hold of a bit of straw, plait it in under your bonnet to make blond hair."

"How much kindling will we be chopping tonight?" asks a voice from the back.

"Only one gate. That's the instruction. This is only the start of the battle. Another gang are getting rid of the gate at Llandeilo; we're doing the same in Llangadog. It's a show of strength. It'll take the pressure off the lads in the west. Things will soon be hotting up in Cwm Gwendraeth and the Loughor valley. The Dragoons are far enough away tonight and they're not going to know where to turn next."

"Which gate is it to be, then?"

"The Glan Sawdde Gate, near the bridge. Bring axes, saws, a sledgehammer, crowbars. It'll be in bits in no time."

"And what about the toll-house?"

"We'll knock in the roof. No one will be able to live in it then."

"Set it on fire, that's what's needed!"

"KNOCK IN the roof," the blacksmith says emphatically.

"Where's Rebecca's white horse, then?"

"Don't you worry about that," Llew says, "I've organised it."

"But I didn't think there was one available round here ..."

"There's one closer than you think," says the smith. "He's

grazing on Coed yr Arlwydd Common at the moment."

"That gyppo pony! We can't put Beca on a pony belonging to one of those—"

"Everyone has a right to travel freely," Llew says, holding up his hand. "The Lee family are part of the traditional way of life in this area. They're with us. And I want to see someone from every family, one from each house, at the Rhyd-y-saint crossroads at midnight. On your way home, call by your neighbours. Tell them that Beca's horn calls. I want to see a big, noisy procession from Rhyd-y-saint to Glan Sawdde."

"Are we to bring arms?"

"Only to fire in the air," the blacksmith says. "There's no other target. Only to create noise and fear. No one disappoints Rebecca, do they, my Daughters?"

"No, Mother!" chorus the voices in the pub, as one.

One of the lads snatches a hunting horn off the wall of the pub and sounds a series of long notes.

"Go home and prepare, my Daughters! Will you be ready?"

"We will, Mother!"

"Will you be noisy, my Daughters?"

"We will, Mother!"

"Will your axes be sharp, my Daughters?"

"They will, Mother!"

And then, laughing and shouting, the customers rise and head for the door.

As they clear the tables, Tegwen Rees has the most to say.

"Men their age playing the fool, going back to dressing up like when they were little lads at Hallowe'en. That's all it is, a bit of play-acting on fair day."

"Mam! It's a serious cause. Families are being turned off their farms ..."

"I know money's tight, Gwyndaf. What it needs is everyone to work a little bit harder and live a little more simply and—"

"They wouldn't come here to the pub for a bit of a laugh then, would they, Mam?"

"We'd be alright," says Tegwen sharply. "We've always looked after ourselves. Oh, and dressing up in women's clothes! Whatever next?"

Just then Elin comes downstairs clutching a bundle of white petticoats and an old woollen shawl.

"Here you are, Dad!" she says as she spreads them over the table. She extracts a bonnet from her apron pocket. "And there's this for your head! Is there a prize for the prettiest Daughter?"

"Brython, you're not going! Tell her!"

Brython sits silently at the table, worrying at the clothes with his fingers.

"No one can offend Beca, and if we do there'll be retribution and it'll affect the pub."

"So which is worse – retribution from Beca or retribution from the church and the authorities? They own the pub and our living, you just remember that!"

"I've got no choice, Tegwen. It's the Daughters of Rebecca who rule the valley tonight."

"Well, if you're going to be a woman, you can jolly well clear these tables yourself tonight!" And with that, Tegwen storms out of the door and marches upstairs.

"Gwyndaf, go and scrape a bit of soot off the back of the big chimney, would you?" Elin says.

Chapter 8

"The constables have been round the village – two of them! They've just gone over Pont Carreg Sawdde."

That's the worrying news Gwyndaf shares after his trip to the shops in Llangadog the following morning.

"Oh! Here we go!" cries his mother. "I knew we shouldn't have gone against the order of things! We should know our place in this old world."

"They're looking for Rebecca who smashed the Glan Sawdde Gate, they are," Gwyndaf says. "And guess what? A gate was smashed to smithereens in Llandeilo last night too. The Walk Gate—"

"—right by the entrance to Dinefwr Park and the Dragoons!" says Elin excitedly.

"Have the clothes Dad was wearing last night been washed?" Gwyndaf asks. "There'd have been splinters from the gate and soot all over them."

"I got up early to wash them," Tegwen says. "They're outside, drying."

"I'll go and fetch them off the line and hide them in the little hut," Elin says. "Petticoats on the line will let the cat out of the bag!"

"The axe he had with him – go and wash it and hide it in the barn under the other tools," Tegwen says to Gwyndaf.

"Mam, you go and give his face another going over with

soap and water," Elin says. "To make sure there's no soot clinging anywhere. Where is he?"

"Down in the cellar. I'll go now ..."

"I'm going to warn Anna and the family," Elin says. "For heaven's sake – the white pony is theirs."

She hurries down the path through the fields to Pont Goch. Nest Morgan is outside the cottage.

"Good morning, Nest. How are you today, and how is Edryd Morgan? Were you disturbed in the early hours by the noise of the horns and shouting in the road?"

"Edryd will be going out shortly. But his leg still pains him. The bone hasn't mended properly. I'm worried that he won't be able to go back to cutting wood. And no, I heard nothing last night – I sleep like a log."

"There are constables in the village. They might come over to question you."

"I heard nothing," Nest says, sticking out her chin defiantly. "And I certainly didn't see anything. Are you sure they came this way?"

She's giving me a dress rehearsal for when the constables come, thinks Elin. She's a good woman, fair play to her.

"I have to get on," Elin says out loud. "Give my regards to Edryd Morgan."

She crosses the road and starts up the rise that leads to the footbridge. She is surprised to see Dan Dowlais out and about so early, walking towards her across the bridge.

"Have the constables left Carreg Sawdde Common yet, Dan?"

"What constables are they, Elin?"

Gwyndaf came home with the news that there were two constables from Carmarthen asking for Rebecca round the village."

"Oh, I wouldn't know about that. I'm just out for a walk to get the smoke from the smithy out of my lungs, I am."

"I'm in a bit if a hurry. Bye!"

Elin and Dan pass each other, she heading for a field below the wooded common. Before stepping onto the bridge, she looks to her right, downriver, and sees that the two mounted constables have already reached the Pont Goch bend. She pauses. She notices that Nest Morgan has disappeared inside the cottage.

Then, to her surprise, she sees Dan Dowlais has stepped off the bridge, has walked down the road and is standing in front of the constables. She thinks to herself, why didn't he wait on the bridge, concealed? There is quite a discussion going on between the blacksmith's son and the officers. She sees Dan turn and point towards Coed yr Arlwydd – and then point at the shaded path linking the road to the footbridge. The two constables dismount.

What an idiot, she thinks, he's directing them to the Lee family. Was he full of spite after being kicked out of the meeting in the pub last night? Elin realises she must warn them without delay. She dashes off the bridge and starts running across the wide field. She manages to remember the guidance Anna had given her during the race on Carreg Sawdde Common.

At the far side of the field, a cart track rises steeply between the trees, up to the common. Elin breathes steadily, shallowly and quickly, and takes small, quick steps until she reaches the fork. She turns to the left and runs along flat ground until she reaches the clearing. The whole gypsy family is there, looking completely unperturbed.

"Constables!" she shouts. "They're on their way here from Pont Goch."

"We're expecting them, Elin *fach*," Jorjo says. "It's nothing out of the ordinary for us to be questioned by constables."

"Big footed *mingries*, they are," adds Mari Lee.

"Did you get stopped by them, Elin?" Anna asks.

"No, I was on the footbridge – on my way to let you know." Elin knew from what her father had said that Jorjo and Tom had joined the Daughters last night. She saw that there was no sign of any clothes drying on the gorse bushes this morning.

"Dicw!" she says. "You'll have to do something about him! They're bound to be making enquiries about a white pony."

"But our Dicw's lame," Jorjo says. "He's been like that since Llanybydder horse fair. I was swindled by some dealer into paying over the odds for a *waffadi* pony."

"They have sovereigns for eyes," Mari says.

"He's been hobbling since Cil-y-cwm. The constables can ask the Dragoons – they saw the state of him on Sunday night when we were on our way to this clearing."

"His hoof's been in forge-water ever since then," Mari says.

They're rehearsing their lines too, Elin thinks.

She turns to look at Dicw and sees that he's tethered to a branch with his hoof in a bucket. She wis pretty sure the water will be tinged with iron.

"I can walk him round the woods to show how lame he is," Tom says.

"But not too far – we don't want the lameness to get worse," Jorjo says.

Elin's eyes widen. How on earth is this possible?

"Leaves that protect us against evil spirits," Mari explains, winking at Elin.

"Holly leaves?"

"Only two little ones. Under the hoof. Not enough to give the animal real pain but they'll make him uncomfortable enough to show he's lame if he puts his weight on them."

"You're ready for them, that's clear!" says Elin. "There's the sound of someone coming up the track through the woods. It's bound to be them. I'll go on up to the road and back to Rhyd-y-saint. I'll see you later."

As she walks home by herself, Elin turns over in her mind everything she has seen. Her thoughts keep coming back to the scene between Dan and the constables. It's plain he was giving them important information. But why? He could have put Jorjo and his family in danger. Lucky they're prepared and have a good story. What's behind it all?

After arriving back at Tafarn y Wawr, she goes to find her father and tells him all she's seen and heard. He's finishing cleaning the public bar.

Brython sits down at one of the tables and rubs his chin.

"There's something different about Dan, ever since he came back from Merthyr and the ironworks," he says, after a moment's pause. "He was there during the troubles twelve years ago when they sent in the yeomanry and infantry against the workers. But ironworkers and miners don't cave in at the first sign of trouble. There was bloodshed. The soldiers fired on the crowd, killing sixteen of them, and one of the soldiers was killed in the violence too. A Welshman, Dic Penderyn, was hung for wounding one of the soldiers – wounding, mark you, not killing – and he was innocent, according to Dan. After it was all over, he came back to Llangadog, but he brought Dowlais back with him. And not only in name. He's concealing something about that time."

As she goes about her chores that morning, what her father has told her about Dan keeps nagging at her. What if the constabulary have some hold over Dan, such that they can squeeze him for information? But Dan was as fired-up about Beca as the next man. But then again, was that just for show? Was that just a way to get himself into the thick of things and collect information? But his own father was Beca in this area! Maybe his game was to divert attention towards others to protect his own father? On the other hand, Dan and his father never worked at the smithy at the same time. Was there some coolness between them? Did Llew Lewis know something about his son's past, maybe? Every question leads to another question in Elin's mind. But the biggest question of all remains – is Dan Dowlais a traitor to the cause of Rebecca? She decides that she must keep a close eye on the blacksmith's son.

After dinner, she decides to go down to Llangadog to see if there's anything to see there. She follows the Cae-rhyn road and then takes the path towards Carreg Sawdde. As she gets closer, she can see from the field path that the Trust's workmen are already erecting a bar across the road next to the toll-house, where the Glan Sawdde Gate had been. She sees that the remains of the old gate might as well be kindling, and that there are small chips of wood scattered up the hedge. It won't be long before tolls start to be collected once more, she thinks.

Three or four other workers are lifting bundles of straw to form a new roof on the toll-house. The husband and wife who open and close the gate will be back at their duties before nightfall, she thinks. Elin recognises the man on a sturdy horse who is overseeing everything and is occasionally pointing to one or two of the workers and barking commands. That brute from the estate: the steward with a neck like a bullock's. What was his name again? Bishop! She smiles as she recalls the crowd at the back of the White Horse jeering at him.

But it's he who is on his high horse today, thinks Elin. Nothing's changed. She looks over in the direction of the bridge over the river Sawdde. She sees that the grumpy little toll-keeper who works the gate beside the bridge is standing outside his door, looking across at the scene. He must have been scared when he heard the horns and guns in the small hours. He was sure to have thought he was for it then. Elin wonders what he had done with his children. She can see them playing happily in the river this afternoon. They probably saw nothing.

There's a man coming over the bridge. Him again – Dan Dowlais. Elin watches the way he walks the length of the road until he reaches its junction with the road from Llangadog to the Black Mountain. He looks up and down the road before turning towards the village. He's going to pass the toll-house, Elin thinks, scarcely believing her own eyes. He's returning to the scene of the riot, and right under the nose of the steward of the big house!

Elin sees Bishop raise his head and look around, still mounted. He looks towards the village and down the road towards Pont Goch. He turns towards the workmen on the roof and barks a few words, and the gang come down, cross the road and start piling the pieces of the old gate into a cart on the other side of the road.

Bishop motions to Dan to go inside the toll-house. He then glances up and down the road before dismounting and disappearing, following Dan.

Elin thinks, what do those two have to discuss?

There is a bend in the hedge between her and the main road, meaning it skims the back of the house. As she gets nearer to Pont Carreg Sawdde, the path joins the road, but Elin turns her steps into another field to bring her towards the hedge and the walls of the toll-house. She can hear the voices of the men inside the small building. Part of the roof is still missing, so she can hear some words clearly now. But they're speaking English! Dan has learned English while working in the ironworks, Elin thinks. She listens attentively but she can't follow the flow of the conversation. Nonetheless, she can tell from the tone that they're not arguing. They are speaking on genial terms, she thinks.

Then she hears a familiar name.

"... Pumsaint ..."

That's what Dan says. The Dragoons had been in Pumsaint. But there was no attack by Beca there. That was a wild goose chase for the Dragoons. Then again, were they expecting that Rebecca and her Daughters would be smashing gates there soon? She concentrates again, but the English words go in one ear and out the other. Then, she picks up another familiar word.

"... tomorrow ..."

Dan is speaking again. The day after today, *yfory*, that's what 'tomorrow' means – Elin knows that much. But what does it all mean? And then another familiar word comes.

"... midnight ..."

The middle of the night, *canol nos*, Elin thinks. She hears Dan's voice get louder, as if he's emphasising the whole thing. "... Pumsaint ... tomorrow ... midnight ..."

And then comes a word that Elin immediately understands the significance of.

"... Rebecca ..."

After all that, she hears a sentence from Bishop, unintelligible to her except for the final word.

"... Go!"

She hears Dan leaving the toll-house. A short while later, she hears Bishop's footsteps leaving and he must have called the workers back to finish the roof because they start to climb the ladders once more.

I must go. I can't be caught hiding here, Elin thinks. She slips out of the field and heads back to the footpath up the slope.

But where can she go? To whom can she tell what she's

just witnessed? One thing is clear to her. If the Daughters of Rebecca are abroad in Pumsaint tomorrow night – and if an attack has been planned – they are in grave danger of being caught.

Chapter 9

Elin doesn't sleep well that night. She tosses and turns in her bed, and the words she heard from behind the toll-house give her a headache. Just before dawn she falls into a restless sleep, full of nightmares. She sees herself mounted on Dicw the pony and galloping across Carreg Sawdde Common, her long blonde hair loose and rippling out behind her in the wind, and fifty Dragoons chasing her, each with his sword drawn. Oh, they look vicious! She gallops towards Llew Lewis' smithy. The blacksmith is standing in front of the smithy with a large hammer in his hand, waving it wildly to urge her to gallop faster. Elin turns the pony towards the river. She sees the bridge ahead of her. But the toll-gate is closed. Someone is coming out of the toll-house – but it's not the little man in the bowler hat. It's Dan Dowlais! And he's refusing to open the gate for her, he's holding his hand out for fourpence! She turns Dicw towards the pool in the river beside the bridge ... but the toll-house children are swimming in it!

She comes to. She opens her eyes. She lies on her back for a while. Should she share with someone what she saw and heard? Gwyndaf? But what could he do? Her father? He didn't want to get dragged into the cause of Beca in the first place – his heart isn't in it. Her mother? No way! Jorjo and his family? Some saw them as outsiders and were suspicious of them.

Llew the blacksmith? He is the Beca of the neighbourhood ...
he and his son had fallen out badly and in public too. But, in
the end, he was Dan's father. Jac from the Plough Inn? But
how on earth would she get the time and the excuse to travel
six miles there and six miles back? The man in the black
cravat ...? She didn't know his name, nor anything else about
him, but he was at the centre of things ...

Elin lay there brooding. There's nothing to be done except
get up and face the day, she says to herself. Something was
bound to show her what path to take, all she had to do was
start doing something instead of lying in bed doing nothing.

Her father is in the yard, hitching up the mare between the
shafts of the cart.

"Where are you going?" she asks him. "Do you want any
help?"

"No, no ... I'll be fine, thanks. You know how it is. Shifting
stuff about from one place to another."

"I could do with a change of scene ..."

"No, it's not the sort of journey where I'd need you, Elin."

"Where are you going, then?"

But Brython just carries on with his preparations without
replying to his daughter.

Elin goes back inside the part of the pub in which the
family lives, and before long she sees her father driving the
cart out of the yard.

"Where's Dad going today, Mam?"

"Oh, just some job for someone else, that's all. Come
and help me with this bread. This dough needs kneading
and it'll be quicker with two. The big oven'll be ready for

baking by the time these have risen."

By the time she's finished with the bread, Elin has made her mind up. She goes off to look for her brother, and finds him in the barn, sharpening scythes in readiness for the coming harvest.

"Come with me, Gwyndaf. I want to go and see Jorjo and his family."

"Well, Dad said he wouldn't be home until late, so I'll have plenty of time to finish these later on."

Gwyndaf puts down the tool he's working on and in no time they're walking together down through the fields.

"Where was Dad going with the cart, then?" Elin asks.

"He didn't really explain. Some job for Richard Chandler, the parish beadle, or something ..."

"The parish?" Elin looks puzzled. "Has he started collecting church tithes or something? That's the job of that Chandler man, isn't it?"

"Yes, but no, not as far as I know. And anyway, these days people pay tithes in money, not in kind – you know, they used to have to give one tenth of their crops."

"Yes, and that's more difficult for many people."

The purpose of their father's secretive mission becomes plain when they arrive at Pont Goch and the cottage. There, they see estate workers carrying furniture out of the cottage and putting it in their father's cart. In the middle of the road, the estate steward is seated on his horse, overseeing proceedings.

"Bishop! I don't believe it! Dad is working for that scoundrel Bishop, of all people!"

"What are they doing?" Gwyndaf asks in confusion. "They're emptying the cottage ..."

His father is holding the mare's reins as the workers load the cart. Beside the back of the cart stands a tall, thin man in a black overcoat. Elin knows that this is Richard Chandler, the beadle of Llangadog parish. Some in the parish call him the Snake. He has a thin, bony face and narrow, narrow eyes, just like a snake's. It is a face that is incapable of smiling. He takes his pleasure from going from farm to farm to collect the church tithe. He enjoys seeing the local Welsh people squirm as they pay their money to the church, even though they are members of chapels. He can understand and speak Welsh well, but has learned it so he can get to know the business of everyone in the parish. He keeps order in the village, grousing at the children and unleashing the sharp edge of his tongue on those who've had a drop too much to drink of a Saturday night or on fair day. Some say he has a cell in the church tower in which he occasionally locks people overnight. It is Richard Chandler who also makes sure paupers are not a burden on the parish.

"Dad! Dad!" yells Elin. "Where are Edryd and Nest Morgan? Why are you clearing the cottage? And why are you here in the first place? Are you helping these ravening wolves to turn two old people out of house and home?"

"Careful what you say now, Elin," her father says, with a look of furious shame. "There's nothing to concern you with what's happening here. I'm only carting—"

"The work of the Devil is the same as the Devil himself, Dad!

"The money that'll come from selling the furniture will go towards caring for Edryd and Nest—"

"Caring for? ... Will they not need furniture where they're going?"

"Elin *fach*, they couldn't pay their rent. There's no hope of Edryd working again ... The estate wants to rent the cottage to someone else ..."

"But Edryd was working for the estate when the tree fell and smashed his leg! And now they get to turn him out of his home. And, worse still, here you are helping them do their dirty work!"

"Hush now, let's have a bit of respect. Look, they're coming out."

Elin can see the couple coming out of the cottage door. They look twenty years older than the last time she'd seen them. By now, Edryd's lameness tilts his whole body and he can't move without leaning heavily on Nest's arm. The pair walk towards a light cart, painted black, that is standing beyond Bishop on his horse.

This is the first time Elin notices the black cart.

"Whose is the black cart, Dad?"

"It's the Llan'dyfri Workhouse's, Gwyndaf says, a lump in his throat. "I've seen it before, taking a family out of the little houses on Church Street."

"Llanymddyfri Workhouse!" Elin spits. "Dad! You're helping those dogs put these two in the workhouse. You traitor!"

"I am not, and don't you ever say that again, my girl," says Brython, his daughter's words having obviously touched a nerve. "I'm nothing to do with the workhouse. I'm carrying furniture and—"

"And taking it to be sold. And where will the money go? Into the pockets of those who run the workhouse in Llan'dyfri. Edryd and Nest won't see a penny."

"It will go to support them – food, accommodation ..."

"They'll be supporting themselves, Dad. Haven't you heard how they treat the paupers? Breakfast at half past six and bed at eight at night, and working ten hours a day. Poor Edryd can't stand but they'll put him on a stool to cut firewood all day, every day ..."

"Well, at least he'll be handling wood, that's what he likes ..."

"And poor Nest will have to have to unravel old, tarred ropes to be used as caulking between the planks of ships – and her fingers will be all cuts and blood and scars, and she'll have rheumatism in her fingers in no time ..."

"But at least they'll get food and they won't starve ..."

"Food, you say, Dad? Watery soup and gruel! But worse than any of this, when they arrive at the workhouse in Llanymddyfri today, Nest will be sent to the room on the left and Edryd to the right. And that'll be that, they'll never see each other again. Never!"

Her father has no repost to that.

"Oh, Dad! How could you stoop so low for a few pennies?"

Elin runs down the road, past the brown suit and bowler hat sitting on his horse, and towards the black cart. She reaches out her hand and places it on Nest's arm. She is sitting on one seat in the back of the cart, facing her husband on the other. The wife raises her head and looks at Elin with cloudy, faraway eyes. Any hope of seeing sunshine in her eyes again have gone forever, thinks Elin. She tries to think of something suitable to say, but her mouth is completely dry.

Nest moves her arm and holds Elin's hand in hers. And squeezes it. Then the old woman starts singing softly and brokenly. Elin has heard the lullaby before, but hasn't taken much notice of the words until today. Every word is like a hammer pounding nails into a coffin.

"Hush a-bye baby, sleep little chick,
Before you get old, before you get sick,
Before you're a debtor, before you get weak
And sent to the poorhouse, then graveyard so bleak."

"Take them away," says a dispassionate voice behind her, from beneath the bowler hat.

The driver of the black cart is already on his seat. He gives the reins a flick and the horse starts on his way. Nest lets go of Elin's hand. Elin looks at them both for the last time – husband and wife, each with a small bundle of clothes at their feet. As the cart moves off, she can hear Nest repeating the song.

"Hush a-bye baby, sleep little chick,
Before you get old, before you get sick,
Before you're a debtor, before you get weak
And sent to the poorhouse, then graveyard so bleak."

* * *

Elin and Gwyndaf are leaning over the handrail of the footbridge, looking down at the river's flow.

Both twins know what the other is thinking without the need for words.

Their father has driven the cart away by now. The steward and his underlings have left. But the singing of the wife of Pont Goch Cottage is still whispering in their ears.

Eventually, Elin lets out a deep sigh.

"He was only doing it to keep the wolf from the door, that's what Dad said, Gwyndaf. But you don't do that by doing the wolf's work, do you?"

Gwyndaf looks her in the eye. He can see the passion in those blue eyes. He can see the pain.

"I agree with you, Elin, every word. Dad has hurt me deeply too. I feel helpless. But you have to remember that we're all only one step away from the workhouse. We're all poor. Mam, Dad and us too. Everyone has to watch every penny."

"But Gwyndaf, isn't it possible to watch out for each other with care too, through all this?"

And with that, Elin straightens up and stops slouching on the handrail.

"I have something to do. Come on."

Gwyndaf follows her off the bridge and into the field.

"Why are we going to see the Lees, Elin?"

"You'll see."

After greeting each other in Coed yr Arlwydd, five of them sit down on rounds of tree trunks serving as stools. Tom has gone to help with the harvest on a farm on the lowlands of the Tywi valley, says his mother.

"I see a black cloud, despite the blue sky," Mari Lee says, looking into Elin's eyes.

This is the opportunity for the girl and her brother to tell all they'd witnessed and share their burden with the family.

"Big men with tiny hearts, they are," says Mari Lee, after hearing about the behaviour of Bishop the steward and Chandler the beadle.

"I can think of a hundred other names for them too," growls Jorjo.

"Outside, the church; inside, the Devil," says Mari Lee.

"But they get their way again and again," Gwyndaf says.

"Look how they even managed to get Dad invested in their cause," Elin says.

"Oh, that's not totally fair, now," her brother replies. "You can't say Dad was invested in what we saw at Pont Goch Cottage."

"Your dad is a servant," says Mari Lee. "Don't point your finger at the servant because of the master's fist. They always achieve their ends, one way or another."

"And it's very likely that he'll achieve his ends by catching Beca at her work tonight!" adds Elin passionately.

"Catch Beca? What makes you say that?" Jorjo shoots back.

She tells him all that she heard while hiding behind the hedge beside the old toll-house on the road to Llangadog, her words tumbling out.

"Could Dan have betrayed Beca, d'you think?" Elin says,

tears of pain running down her face by now. "Bishop could have given a message to the Dragoons, and hundreds of the Daughters will be cut to pieces by their swords tonight. They could even catch Beca herself! What hope will there be then for the people round here?"

Jorjo stands up.

"Some foxes run ahead of the hounds," he says, "but the craftiest foxes escape before the hounds are up. We need to think boldly. The hounds haven't closed in for the kill yet. I think Jac at the Plough is our best bet. We'll take the message to him.

"The inn of salmon and sewin," says Mari Lee.

"Yes, he has been known to pay for the odd fish that happened to jump out of the river Tywi into my hands," says Jorjo quietly. "He knows what hospitality is. And he's always in the thick of things."

"He said something on the day of the fair at Llandeilo about carrying messages from link to link along a chain," Elin says.

"I'll go on Dicw over the hill to Dan-yr-allt and through the ford at Rhyd-y-Saeson," Jorjo says. "And I know the way through the fields to avoid the gates at Rhosmaen."

After the gypsy has left without delay, Elin stands up and so does Gwyndaf, but they both feel as if they don't know what to do with themselves.

"I don't much feel like going home," says Gwyndaf, wholly in tune with his sister's mood. "It'll be difficult passing Pont Goch Cottage again."

"The feet can shift bad thoughts," Mari Lee says. "Come

on down to the field among the trees. You come too, Anna."

"What are you on about?" Gwyndaf asks.

"Running," says the woman, rising nimbly to her feet. "How do you get information to travel far and travel fast? Information about something that you can't trust to anyone else. Information that you must carry yourself."

The others look at her in silence.

"You run it!" Mari says, flashing a smile. "Come with me down to the field below the common."

"Take off your clogs and wear them on your hands like gloves," Mari Lee says, once they have reached the meadow surrounded by a thick belt of trees, hidden from the world.

She sets to, encouraging them and sharing one or two points of technique.

"Bend the knees as you run ... keep your feet in line with your hips ... you're closer to the earth like that ... you're less likely to fall ... small steps ... long strides damage your heels ... a light bounce off the ground ... land on the outer edge of the ball of your foot ... short breaths ... not too deep ... Come on now, let's see you run once round the field ... and again ... and again ..."

Chapter 10

The following afternoon, Elin manages to get away from work in the pub. The heavy silence between her and her parents was getting to be too much. She decides to go up the back road behind the pub, towards the hills. She makes for Pantmeinog and soon finds herself running, even though she is wearing her clogs. Once there, she follows Nant Dyrfal down towards Coed Glansefin. She pulls off her clogs and shoves her hands in between the leather and the wooden soles. She feels released as she runs freely and smoothly.

She runs through the woods, down the slope. She feels pain in her knees as she tries to brace her legs to stop herself falling, and her feet hit the ground heavily as she tries to keep her balance. I can't go for long like this, she thinks. There must be an easier way to run downhill. She'll have to ask Mari Lee for advice.

Fortunately, is isn't a long hill. She reaches the bottom and emerges from the wood onto the level road past the Glansefin stables. She turns towards Llangadog, running easily now. She speeds up and feels liberated. She leaves the road and takes a field path to the left, in the direction of Glan Sawdde farm. After crossing three fields, she sees the earth mound of Castell Meurig, Llangadog's old castle, on her left, only a field's width away. She turns and runs up the slope. She picks her steps carefully as the ground rises towards her.

A step to the left, then to the right to avoid a rough bit and then a bounce to move on ... using the fronts and sides of her feet. She's out of breath by the time she reaches the wooded top, but she smiles as she holds her sides.

After a short while, she straightens up and turns to look at the view. She can see the three valleys of the three rivers – Sawdde, Brân and Tywi – all joining a little below Pont ar Dywi. The countryside is endless fields. She sees that, in places, haymaking has started – there are armies of mowers with their scythes cutting the grass into swathes. Her father had said that they'd be starting on their haymaking tomorrow, too. What a lovely country, she thinks.

She looks down on the common along the Sawdde riverbank. There are a lot of animals grazing the common at this time of year – farmers have moved their cattle from grassed fields to the common land. She'd always known this, somehow, having been raised with the practice. Although none of the people on the common own it, they all have the right to use it. She wonders how this could be, but it also all makes sense to her. The farmers and villagers all share the common, and share it with the gypsies who come to camp there as well, of course. Everyone could take water from the river and fish it from the common. She can see that there are children in the pool beside the bridge this afternoon.

Elin starts running again. Back to the footpath, and this time she tries going two steps to the right and two to the left as she goes downhill. It's easier on the knees than pushing off heavily in a straight line, one heel and then the next. Although she takes more steps as she follows a zigzag path, she feels she's running faster.

She follows the path to Glan Sawdde farm, on past the barrier that has replaced the gate next to the toll-house, and takes a right for the common. She crosses Pont Carreg Sawdde and heads for the next gate.

"Do you want me to open the gate?" a little voice shouts from beside the toll-house.

Elin looks at a small, barefoot girl aged about five.

"Hello there, how are you?" she says to her. "And what's your name?"

"Rachel."

"And are you going to open the gate for me, like a big girl?"

"Yes, you do it like this."

Rachel reaches up on tiptoe and unhooks the gate's catch.

"Thank you very much, Rachel!" Elin smiles as she passes her. "You're an expert at this."

Her father comes to the door in his black bowler hat. He doesn't smile, nor say a word.

"Are you running on the common today?" asks Rachel.

"Yes, a bit."

"But there's no race, is there?"

"No, no racing today."

"Can I run with you then?"

"Of course you can. We'll run along the riverbank this way, shall we?"

"Yeeeeay!" the little girl squeals excitedly.

"Oh, can I run with you too, Rachel?" Elin sees another

girl, about a year older, splashing her way out of the river and joining them.

"And who are you, then?"

"Mei. Rachel's big sister."

"And me! And me!" cries a skinny little boy playing happily on the riverbank.

"And who are you?"

"Dafy."

"He's our little brother," Rachel says. "He can't run fast yet. He's only four."

"It doesn't matter! You can all come!"

The four of them run alongside the river Sawdde. Elin slows her speed so as not to push the children too hard. They're giving it everything, arms and legs flying. And laughing and smiling at the same time. She notices that their steps go left and right naturally. They're all barefoot too, and she sees them arch the soles of their feet as they meet the ground.

"Make a rainbow with your feet!" That was Mari's advice to her, Elin remembers.

And, most importantly of all, they're enjoying themselves. Running isn't something serious, painful. They're having a great time. More than that, thinks Elin – they're running as if they've heard Mari Lee's advice – bending their legs, feet squarely under their hips, keeping the body low.

"First to the bend in the river!" Elin shouts, hanging back so that Dafy comes third. After the race they end up rolling in the grass and screaming and laughing fit to burst!

How lovely to be like this, thinks Elin. Then Elin spots Jorjo walking across the common with Abram, the runner who raced them. They stop and stand by the tent of a tall, thin man with dark hair and two gold rings through one ear. The weight of the world descends once more onto her shoulders.

"You carry on playing running," she says to the family of little ones. "I'll come back to have a race with you another day."

She walks towards the three men and as she gets closer Jorjo gestures to her to join them.

"This is Edmund, Abram's father," he explains. "He's just come back from Talley and he called in at the Plough. He's got a good story."

Her spirits rise when she sees Jorjo smiling. Maybe it's good news after all. She dares to hope.

"I had a word with Jack at the Plough," Edmund says. "I told him who I was."

He casts a glance at Jorjo as he says this.

"Jac knows full well who he can trust, Edmund," Jorjo says.

"Thanks to Jorjo, the message that the Dragoons were on their way to Pumsaint at midnight had arrived in time."

"And thanks to Elin here too, without her I wouldn't have got the warning," Jorjo says.

"As luck would have it, the Daughters had arranged to meet earlier. They were gathering at nine o'clock at the fork in the road where one road goes to Llanwrda and Talley and the other goes to Pumsaint. There was no hanging about. On to the task in hand, Beca said. There were hundreds there and plenty of weapons. Off they went at a trot to the Ynysau Gate, this side of Pumsaint, and in just a few minutes the wood there was reduced to chips only fit for bedding animals. Then they set the toll-house on fire—"

"Set the house on fire! But what about the people that lived there?"

"They'd been warned, according to Jac. But the toll-keeper was such an idiot. He was speaking English and trying to get money out of everyone who was on horseback. He hadn't got a clue, and he was so supercilious. He won't be at his gate again ..."

"What time was it by then?" asks Elin.

"Someone had said it was only just ten o'clock, and 'Let's get on with the work!' someone else said. So off they went, parading through Pumsaint, sounding their horns and firing their guns in the air."

"No one ventured out of their houses after that and so no one can give testimony that they recognised any of the gang," Jorjo explains.

"The Glan Twrch turnpike is the other side of Pumsaint. Do you remember the gate across the road there?"

The other two men nod.

"Well it's not there any more!"

"And what about the toll-house? And the family?"

"Oh, this toll-keeper was more of a gentleman. When Rebecca, at the head of the crowd, asked if she could come through the gate, he says – the toll-keeper, mind – says 'Of course you can, Mother. I won't charge you a penny!' And a big 'hooray' went up from the crowd. The man went back indoors to his family. He was instructed to close the door and the curtains, and although the gate was in splinters in minutes, nothing unfortunate happened to the house or its roof or anyone in it."

"And were the Dragoons on their way or not?" Elin asks.

"Don't rush him, *croten*!" Jorjo smiles. "Let him tell the story in his own time. He's enjoying himself!"

"'Clear the road!' That's what Beca shouted after the work on the gate was done. Everyone spread out and moved back about half a mile away from the toll-house then: some went into the woods and some crossed the river. And everyone was to be still. Rebecca didn't want hundreds of people walking along noisily, you see, or the Dragoons would hear them. Ten minutes after that – only ten minutes, mark you – the Dragoons could be heard coming over into the valley. They saw the fire in the first toll-house and they went wild, drawing those long swords out in front of them ... through Pumsaint like hellhounds and then they stopped at the second toll-gate ... Bear in mind, now, there were hundreds of Daughters behind the hedges, in the fields and on the slopes above, each one as still as a statue and no one making a sound ... The captain of the Dragoons started shouting then, telling the toll-keeper to come out ... and out he came, looking very worried, shoulders hunched and eyes darting everywhere ... The captain must have asked him which way Rebecca and her Daughters had gone ... and you know what?"

Edmund pauses for dramatic effect, or to catch his breath.

"No! What?" Elin's eyes are alight as she devours every word of the story.

"The toll-keeper pointed up the valley and the road towards Lampeter! In the wink of an eye, the Dragoons were galloping hell for leather towards Lampeter and the Daughters got to go home quietly and safely. And there you have it – the story of last night."

"*Dordi*! Well, I never!" Jorjo says, turning to Abram. "Thank you for coming up to our camp to fetch me so I could hear your dad's story."

"And Jac wanted me to thank you ... both of you," says Edmund, turning to face Elin too. "It's just as well the hedges have ears, that's what he said. And it's just as well the ears side with Beca!"

"Are you going back up to Coed yr Arlwydd?" Elin asks Jorjo. "I've got a couple of questions for Mari Lee about this running business."

"You go on up, *croten*," Jorjo says. "I'm going over to see Llew at the smithy first. I'll be with you later."

When Elin reaches the clearing, Mari and Anna are preparing *cawl*.

"We have coney stew tonight," Mari Lee says.

"Rabbit," explains Anna. "Tom's been catching them in snares. There's a plague of them under the hedges along Nant Geidrych."

"This is what's bothering me about this running thing, Mari Lee. I can run easily on the flat and running uphill doesn't tax me much when I follow what you told me. But coming downhill's a problem. Oh, my body swings and jerks and I get a shooting pain running down from my knees to my heels. How are you supposed to run downhill?"

"That's the most important thing about running cross-country," says Mari Lee. "You can really do a lot of damage to yourself if you're not careful. It's better to take a longer, less steep route. Don't take a straight line and bash your heels into the ground on a hill. It doesn't do the mountain any good – and it makes your heels sore. Keep your legs bent and be light on your feet. Why don't you two to go up the Ceidrych valley now – there's good slopes to practise on there."

The girls look at each other and nod.

"You can have *cawl* made from the hopping *shushi* when you get back. It'll be good for your feet. Take her up the top of Garn Goch, Anna," says Mari Lee, pointing at a rocky hilltop above the hills and woods of the Ceidrych valley.

"Remember – breathing is what it's all about. Breathe into your gut!"

They disappear into the woods.

Within the hour they are back – tired, thirsty and sweaty. But they are both smiling.

"Were your heels painful or were they alright?" Mari Lee asks, handing them each a bowl of rabbit stew.

"No, they're fine, thanks. Tip-top." Elin smiles at her.

The *cawl* is delicious and in no time Mari is giving her a second bowlful. Half way through eating that one, Elin suddenly stops.

"I wonder what they're having for supper in Llanymddyfri Workhouse tonight?"

Chapter 11

The weather is gorgeous in Carmarthenshire the first week of July that year. The scythes are kept busy in the hayfields all the long, sunny days and whole families work at tedding and turning the hay to dry it. The sweet smell of haymaking fills the valleys.

Elin and Gwyndaf are tedding the new-mown hay in one of Tafarn y Wawr's fields one afternoon when a boy rushes in through the open gate to the road, waving his arms wildly.

"What does he want, Gwyndaf?"

"I don't know, but he's calling us over."

"D'you know him?" Elin says, leaving her pitchfork and starting to walk towards the runner.

"No. He's run a long way, by the look of him."

When they get closer to him, the runner gasps out his message.

"The ... the D ... the ... the Drag ...".

"Breathe deeply," Elin tells him. "One ... two ... three ... That's better."

The runner's breathing slows and he manages to get his words out.

"The Dragoons are in Llan'dyfri!"

"Yes, so? They're back and forth every other day, aren't they," says Gwyndaf. "Night and day, they're looking for Beca and her Daughters and trying to learn the country roads."

"No, you don't understand. This isn't the lot that come for the day. These have come from Brecon. They're going to be staying in Llan'dyfri ..."

"Staying? Stationed there you mean?" Elin asks.

"Yes, they're right among us, watching us, trying to turn some of us into traitors when we see their guns and swords."

"Who are you, then?" asks Gwyndaf.

"Ifan from Tynewydd, Myddfai."

"Oh yes, I know Cwm Tynewydd," says Gwyndaf. "What's the name of the son at Ysguborfawr?"

"Emrys."

"Which way did you come?" asks Elin.

"Through the Brân valley and past yr Olchfa and then through Coed Cae'r Bedw ... but then I got lost. I came past Maes Glas ..."

"Who is it you want to see, then?" Elin asks.

"Llew Lewis the Smithy on—"

"—on Carreg Sawdde Common. Yes, I know him," Elin says. "And what's the whole message? You can't run another step, by the looks of you. You've run four miles already."

Ifan was lying on a pile of hay, massaging his legs and still breathing heavily.

"The Dragoons have reached Llan'dyfri. There to stay. No Beca tonight. That's the message. A runner brought the message to me all the way from Llan'dyfri and I was told to take it onward to Llew."

"I'll take the message," Elin says.

"Elin ... would it be better if I went?" Gwyndaf says.

"No, you take Ifan into the house to have something to

drink. He's run four miles." A mischievous smile spreads across Elin's face. "And anyway, I'm faster than you! And you're needed to spread this hay out."

Elin takes off her clogs and starts running towards the gate, across the hay already raked into windrows.

* * *

As she reaches the smithy on the common, Elin notices there are two horses she doesn't recognise in the yard. She slows her pace and sees that Dan Dowlais is working at the forge. He raises his head when her shadow falls across the threshold."Ah, the publican's daughter," he says. "Are those taps holding up or do you have beer flooding the cellar floor?"

"No, they're fine. Is there someone with Llew?"

Dan turns and glances behind him, towards the door to the stable.

"Yes. Two men from Carmarthen. Two newspapermen. But you can go and join them. Maybe you have a story for them, eh?"

Elin looks thoughtfully at Dan for a second. Is he playing cat and mouse with her? Is he trying to extract some information from her? He'd get nothing out of her, she knew that.

"Don't look so scared! There's nothing to be afraid of. They're only collecting facts! Go on in."

"This is Elin from Tafarn y Wawr, this is!" Llew Lewis says, after Elin has knocked shyly on the door and poked her head round it. "Come in, Elin. I'm sure you'd like to hear what these two gentlemen have to say. This is—"

"I've already met Elin."

Elin looks towards the voice for the first time and sees it belongs to Dylan Lloyd, the journalist from the *Carmarthen Journal*.

"Yes, at the fair in Llandeilo," Elin says, nodding an acknowledgement.

"And you're carrying your clogs ... Is it something urgent, Elin?"

"Yes, Llew – a message for *you*." She stresses the last word to hint that it's not something to be shared publicly.

"Dylan Lloyd here is translating into English as we go what we have to share with Thomas Foster. Thomas Foster is from London ..."

Elin turns her head and realises she has seen this man too.

"Didn't he go into the important meeting with you, Dylan Lloyd, the one in the Shire Hall in Llandeilo?"

"Yes, that's him," Dylan says. "You've got a good memory for faces."

"Thomas Foster has items about Carmarthenshire every day in the paper he writes for in London," says Llew. "They've told me this morning that twenty thousand read that paper daily! Twenty thousand, Elin – imagine! Twenty thousand people and every one of them reads the paper!"

"He's written articles about the disturbances, of course," Dylan says. "But he's also interviewed farmers and people walking along the roads. He talks to everyone and collects their stories. I ask his questions for him and then translate the answers."

"What did he have to say in the Shire Hall, then, that Rice-Davies from Dinefwr Park?"

"He's been saying a lot recently," answers Dylan Lloyd. "In Llandeilo, and up and down the county, and he says that he thinks the world of his tenants and his tenant farmers. He's had such a warm welcome in their homes, he says ..."

"Huh! Tea and Welsh cakes it'll be, for the son of the Lord Dynevor," Llew says mockingly.

"He's very sorry to see soldiers used against his own people, but he says anyone creating trouble will lose his home," Dylan goes on to say. "And worse than that, he's warning them that the courts will sentence them to transportation. They'll be clapped in chains and sent on ships to Australia, to prison camps there where they'll have to do hard labour, and they'll never see their homes, their families or Carmarthenshire ever again. If they must, they'll shoot every man in the county. He's doing his best to strike fear into people."

"We're common country folk, we are," says Llew. "We just want to live in peace, to work and earn our living and be with our families. That's all we want. But people have had enough. By now there's fire in the belly of country people."

"We've just been in Merthyr," Dylan says. "There's been fire in the works there for years – and I'm not talking about the fire in the furnaces either. The workers in Glamorganshire have been living under very difficult conditions in the towns and villages where there's heavy industry. These days they feel oppressed and half-starved, and they're ready to fight back too. Maybe they're wilder than country folk – their clubs in the Merthyr area are buying guns and bayonets and bullets. They say there's thousands of workers ready to fight to change things."

"So you see, Elin – you're amongst friends here," says the blacksmith. "These ears listen and put our complaints in papers that reach people in London. Important people in London. So tell me your message, *croten.*"

"A runner brought it from Tynewydd, Myddfai," Elin says. "The Dragoons are stationed in Llan'dyfri. They have arrived from Brecon. There should be no Rebecca tonight. That's the message. He'd lost his way and so I've brought you the message, Llew."

"There should be no Rebecca tonight?" says a voice from the doorway. Elin looks up quickly on hearing the voice of Dan Dowlais repeating her words from the door to the smithy.

"We'll send out the runners," Llew says. "They'll know what to do. The furthest first. Go and tell the son of the woollen mill boss, Dan. He's the one to run the first two miles to get the message to Jac at the Plough."

Dylan turns to the London correspondent and translates this latest news for him. Elin sees him writing notes in a book on his lap.

"They say there's a hundred and fifty constables from London on their way to Carmarthenshire," Dylan tells them. "And that five hundred infantry are coming from Swansea. The government in London thinks the iron fist is the only way to deal with the people's grievances. And they're trying to divide and rule – Rice-Trevor has offered three hundred pounds for information about any ringleader that's organising the destruction of a gate here in West Wales."

"Three hundred pounds!" says Dan Dowlais, popping his head back round the door.

"Thought you were on your way to the woollen mill!" says the smith to his son.

"Just going."

"But there are signs that the message is reaching the right people," Dylan says. "More than one of the Trusts in this county has taken a step back. They've dropped the tolls to the levels they were six years ago in some areas. But it's made no difference to the attacks. Beca and hundreds of her Daughters have been targeting turnpike gates in one place while the Dragoons have been galloping around like mad things looking for them somewhere miles away. It's as if Beca is able to read the minds of the military ..."

"Destroying the gates draws attention," Llew says. "But we need to draw attention to the root of the problem."

"Yes, this poverty," agrees Elin. "No one would want to live in a toll-house and collect money at the gates if it wasn't for poverty."

"Jac from the Plough has called a big meeting for everyone in the area in the burial ground of the chapel in Cwmifor before the end of the month," Llew tells Dylan. "If you can get there, it'll be a chance for you both to hear the experiences and losses we're suffering today. We've reached the end of our tether. Tell him that."

Dylan conveys the message to Thomas Foster and, when he replies, it is clear he has a number of questions. Elin observes that he thinks carefully before asking, and then asks in a steady, dispassionate voice. This one's seeking the truth, she thinks.

"Mr Foster is very keen to be at the meeting and ask questions. What's the date?"

"Thursday the twentieth of July, half past nine at night. Cwmifor is a hamlet in the hills off the main road from Llandeilo to Llan'dyfri, between Rhosmaen and Maenordeilo. As you go up the valley, you'll see a little chapel on the left. It's the Baptist chapel, above the wood and within sound of the stream."

"He's asking if there'll be any objection to him, from London, coming into the middle of something for local people."

"Anyone who wants to be there and listen to us will be welcome."

"And he's asking if there'll be the opportunity to interview people individually – with me asking the questions on his behalf in Welsh."

"Yes, yes. We'll make sure of that. We'll have thought who could share their experiences. A word spoken from the heart is often better than speechifying, isn't it?"

Dylan nods and confirms with the correspondent. He nods his head very definitely. Then both journalists get up – they have to get back to Carmarthen before nightfall, they say.

As he passes Elin, Dylan smiles at her.

"Your feet must be very sore these days!"

Elin feels her cheeks reddening and she bends down

suddenly and puts on the clogs she's been carrying.

"It's the message that's important, not my feet," she says.

"Yes, but the message has to have legs to carry it."

"Or print on paper, maybe," Elin replies. "We read your column every week."

"Well, just make sure you're not *in* the column – nor the headlines," Dylan says. "A girl, a bit younger than you, has just been convicted of leading the rioters from room to room to wreck Carmarthen Workhouse the day of the big demonstration."

"Someone shopped her, did they?"

"Yes, I should think so. But you didn't hear it from us, you understand?"

"Wait here in the stable for a minute," Llew says to Elin. "We'll have a quick word after they've gone."

The three men go out through the smithy to the yard where the horses are waiting. Elin feels in her bones that she will be meeting the two newspapermen again in the near future.

Chapter 12

"So, do you see Elin – we have to be able to get messages from place to place faster than the Dragoons' horses can gallop?"

Llew had just been explaining to her that Beca must be craftier when it comes to making arrangements about nocturnal gatherings at the gates.

"We've been forewarning the toll-keepers, saying exactly which nights we'll be striking. Well, that'll be like issuing an invitation to the Dragoons to be there with a welcoming tea party for us."

"What are you going to do, then?"

"The warning will still be given – but Beca will strike at that gate a week after the date on the paper."

"And the Dragoons will have been there at the earlier date?"

"Yes, they will. On that night, Beca will have had her axe in a gate twenty miles away."

"So, you'll get messages exchanged from places miles apart from each other?"

"Yes. But we'll have to change our tricks all the time. That Love – commandant of the overall army that's now in these counties – he's not thick. We'll only be able to hoodwink him once with each plan. And now, with the Dragoons stationed at Llan'dyfri, six miles from here, we'll have to tighten up the way we work."

"What does that mean, Llew?"

"It means we have to have more runners. A runner every two miles. We would be able to get a message from Llan'dyfri to Llandeilo quicker than the Dragoons on their horses if we have five good runners going cross-country – two miles each, and the message getting transferred from one to the other. They must be fast and know the countryside like the backs of their hands. That way, fleet feet will be mightier than sharp swords."

"Do you have enough, Llew?"

"I'm looking at one now."

"Me! Oh, no. I couldn't be a runner for Beca, Llew! I'm just a girl ..."

"Looking for men dressed as women, they are. They're not going to pay much heed if they come across a girl."

"What will Dad say?"

"I'm yet to meet a girl that couldn't wrap her father round her little finger."

"Mam then. She's dead set against this Beca business ..."

"You leave your mother to me."

"But I've never run two miles – at least not at top speed."

"That's why it's important you practise. Tafarn y Wawr is perfect. It's outside the village, on a quiet country road without toll-gates – and that's valuable in itself. The drovers gather there – so there's always news coming in, and there are paths and lanes going in all directions from it. How would you go to Llan'dyfri from home?"

"Up to Maes Glas, down through the woods to Glansefin and onwards on the road ..."

"... until you come to Llwyn Ifan Feddyg. That's two miles for you. The son at Llwyn Ifan is a runner. He'll be the next link in the chain."

"And where will he run to?"

"You don't need to know. I'm not keeping things from you, just protecting you. You don't need to know and knowing would be a burden. Now, how would you go from Tafarn y Wawr to Llanddeusant?"

"Up Cwm Llwyn-y-bedw ..."

"Then keep going up towards the mountain, over the ridge and then you get to a little lane that takes you to Coed-y-brain. Two miles. Then a fresh pair of legs to carry the message onwards."

"That's a steep mountain."

"You can practise for that. How would you go towards the Black Mountain?"

"Cross-country to Caefylchi then past Caeau Bychain, cross the Ffinnant and then the lane along the slope ..."

"... to Pant-y-grafog. We've got a runner there too. How would you go to Capel Gwynfe and Llandybïe?"

"Rhyd-y-saint ..."

" ... and to Carregfoelgam. Two miles. Or the other road, the one to Ffair-fach as far as Tal-y-garn. What about Llandeilo?"

"Cross the ford at Rhyd-y-Saeson ..."

"And we have a runner at Glan-Rhyd-y-Saeson. So you see, you're two miles in every direction. It's not Tafarn y Wawr, it's Tafarn y World. Your pub is the centre of our world."

"But what do I say if I get stopped by someone? A

constable, maybe, or someone from Newton House – or, worse still, the Dragoons?"

"*Jiw, jiw*, just say a drover who's staying with you is looking for another drover to take some cattle to England ..."

"But Llew, what hope of making any difference to things has an ordinary *croten* like me? The wealth, the law – it's all on their side. And now they've got the swords of the Dragoons too."

"What hope is there for doing anything to change things?" says the blacksmith. "It's not in our nature to lie down and take everything that's thrown at us, Elin *fach*. Not suffering in silence. Not take the abuse and bow our heads, bend our backs. No, putting one foot in front of the other – that's hope. Stepping forward. Going a mile. Going two miles. Running faster than the swords. That's how we'll succeed. Sometimes an ordinary *croten* has to be an extraordinary young woman."

* * *

Between the harvest and the running, the next few days flew by for Elin. Each day, she managed to travel to one of the farms listed by the blacksmith. She wasn't sure of the way every time, but she was pleased of the opportunity to get to know the area better. She noticed cottages she'd never seen before. She aimed her steps at particular trees on hillsides. She chanted the names of the farms to the rhythm of her feet on the path.

She feels the soles of her feet hardening and her breathing and speed improving. She can climb steep slopes without feeling a burning in her lungs. She keeps her eyes two steps ahead of her feet as she goes downhill.

Within the family, only Gwyndaf knows what she's up to. She and her father have avoided eye contact ever since she left him outside Pont Goch Cottage. They speak via Seren the mare during the harvest and while making the haystack at the back of the barn.

"One load more today, is it, Seren?" Elin would say.

"Tell her there's two loads left on the field, Seren," her father would reply.

The following day, it might be, "It's a beautiful morning, Seren. Shall we go up to Cae Pella?" from her father, as he stands in the yard.

"Oh, Cae Pella's the field we're going to today, is it Seren?"

Her mother offers even fewer words. But then again, Elin is seldom in the house these days. She sleeps there, of course, but with the days so long and the weather so fine, she doesn't come home until she's ready to go straight upstairs to her bedroom. Between the farm work and the running, sleep isn't a problem for Elin, but the early dawns wake her.

She tries to turn her back to the light streaming through the window and drop off again, but it isn't easy. She's restless during these hours, dozing but with her sleep filled with strange and fantastical dreams. She wakes frequently in the middle of these dreams, so the course of the dream is often vivid in her mind. Too vivid sometimes.

That morning Elin sees herself running through bracken up a hillside. There is a narrow valley below her and she's running from the shadow into sunlight, with her feet caressing the earth, lightly kissing the grass. The stalks barely bend under her feet, she's running so buoyantly. She leaves no print, as Mari Lee would say.

Then suddenly there's a snake in her path. An adder curled up, sleeping in the sun. Because she's running so lightly, the snake hasn't felt any vibration through the ground as she approaches. Elin almost treads on it, but at the last second it raises its head.

Elin freezes with one leg in the air. She sees the angry face of the snake and is afraid. She looks around for something with which to poke it out of the way. And then, in the dream, Elin sees the snake's head rising up and rising up in front of her, and it grows arms and legs and the head grows bigger still – only the eyes remain the same. Richard Chandler, the beadle of Llangadog parish stands before her now!

Elin turns and starts running down the hill. Not zig-zagging, not treading carefully and deliberately, but like a charging bull. Snake-eyes runs after her, trying to catch her ...

She turns her foot awkwardly ... trips ... then falls headlong ...

And wakes up with the bedclothes in a knot and her heart thumping.

She's had this dream before. Why does this one keep coming back to persecute her?

She gets up and goes out in front of the pub to look at the dawn breaking over the Black Mountain. No one else is up. She starts to run. Her feet carry her. She doesn't know what her feet have in mind for her.

She realises before long that she's on the footbridge beside Pont Goch. She doesn't remember passing the cottage.

She knows where she's going now.

As she reaches the clearing, Mari Lee is holding out a bowlful of some infusion taken from her cooking pot.

"Did you hear my footsteps as I ran through the wood, Mari Lee?"

"No, but I knew you were on your way."

By now, Elin doesn't bother asking the gypsy how she knows such things. She accepts that Mari has stronger-than-ordinary senses.

"Couldn't get to sleep properly, Elin?"

"No, couldn't wake up properly."

"Amounts to the same thing."

"Tell me, Mari Lee, is there any meaning to our dreams?"

"They're not true, but there's truth within them."

"Do you sometimes dream you're running?"

"Yes."

"Running like a child? Running happily?"

"Oh yes, like a breeze over the land. Running like sunlight on a patch of field. Running like a white cloud in a blue sky."

"I have those dreams too, Mari Lee."

"That's because you've learned to love running. It takes us back to the original nature of humans. My ancestors came from far off lands, hot lands, and running was part of their nature. Lived to run, ran to live."

"That's how you know the secrets of how to run properly? And that's why you're teaching me?"

"I was taught by older women in the family. Women can run better than young men, did you know that?"

"Does having to run in fear account for that?"

"Running away from the tiger, running away from the bear you mean? Yes, and running away from bears on two legs as well. But you can't run from some things, it's not even worth trying."

They sit for a long time in front of the tent, sipping the infusion from the bowls.

"What's in this concoction, Mari Lee?"

"Navelwort and bilberries. They're bursting with goodness and will strengthen your blood, Elin."

"It's strength in my legs I need for this running lark."

"No, you need strength in your blood first, *croten*."

Mari Lee stands up and raises her head.

"Someone's coming, and they're in a hurry," she says.

She hears the sound of clumsy feet pounding through the woods. Gwyndaf appears, his cheeks flushed.

"I thought you'd be here," he says, after catching his breath. "Arwel Glan-Rhyd-y-Saeson came over, into the yard and called for you. I got up before Mam and Dad. He's got a message for you. Iori at the Plough has seen them with his own eyes. Dragoons. Some of them are billeted in the King's Head, and their horses are in his stable. Fifty of them arrived in Llandeilo last night. They're all billeted in the town."

"The valley is narrowing," Mari Lee says. "But the narrower the valley, the swifter the water runs."

Chapter 13

"Midnight. The Efail-fach. Under Garn Goch."

That was the message on the afternoon of Saturday the fifteenth of July.

"Three parts to the message," says Llew, standing in the stable at the back of the smithy on the common. "Think of three trees on top of a hill. Think of the three arches of Pont ar Dywi. Think of the three rivers flowing into one: the Tywi, Brân and Sawdde. It's easier to remember things in threes."

Elin nods to indicate that she understands and will remember. She repeats the message quietly to herself.

"There seems to be a pattern with the Dragoons in Llandeilo and Llan'dyfri, too," says the blacksmith. "They might be clever, but it's easy to see what they're doing. Iori from the Plough says that a patrol of two dozen leaves Llandeilo every night at eight, and it goes down the Tywi valley. They sometimes go in the direction of Nantgaredig and return through Llanarthne. They have another circuit towards Llandybïe and another towards Gors-las and Llannon. Then another patrol comes up the valley, heading for Talyllychau – what they call 'Talley' – or Llansawel and sometimes towards Llangadog and onwards up the Sawdde valley towards the gates on the Black Mountain. The Dragoons at Llan'dyfri do the same thing. They've got their routes, you see. There's a pattern to it. Iori Plough Inn has got to know their routine by now and he gets to hear if there's any last-minute change."

"So they won't be out on the road alongside the river, between Llangadog and Ffair-fach?"

"No, they won't."

"They won't be there tonight?"

"No, they won't, *croten*. We've had word. A runner came through the ford half an hour ago."

"Are you sure?"

"As sure as I'm certain that night follows day. Why are you so anxious?"

"I feel it's a lot on my shoulders, Llew. It's me who's taking the message to them. And ..."

"What?"

"And Gwyndaf will be with you tonight. He'll be there representing Tafarn y Wawr."

"Not your father, then?"

"He's poorly. The dust at harvest time affects his breathing. He can't walk far, let alone run if he needs to."

"You'd better start running, then. And remember ..."

"Yes?"

"I don't want to see you with your brother at Efail-fach."

"Oh ... but I'm part ..."

"You are. But your part is to run. We can't afford to lose you. You have to steer clear. Understand?"

"Yes."

"Do you remember the three parts to the message?"

"Midnight. The Efail-fach. Under Garn Goch."

"Good girl! Off you go, then."

"As she walks out through the smithy, Dan Dowlais is giving a piece of metal a good whack on the anvil.

"Which gate is it tonight, then?"

"Midnight. The Efail—"

"Yes, yes," he says impatiently, "I know what the message is. Which gate are they going on to afterwards? That's what I want to know."

"That's not part of the message."

"No, I know – but you're bound to know. He tells you everything, *croten*."

"The Daughters will all find out at midnight. Good luck!"

She turns to leave the smithy but there is a dark silhouette between her and the daylight outside.

"Luck?" queries the tall, thin figure before her.

Hearing the growling voice, she realises who the man in front of her is. Richard Chandler, the parish beadle.

"There's no such thing as luck," says the official. "There's a good life or there's a bad life. Work gets done correctly or it gets done poorly. There's no luck involved."

Elin freezes, wondering if he has heard more of the conversation than that.

"The vicar is asking when the gate will be ready, Dan."

Elin is thankful the beadle has turned away from her by now. A certain coldness creeps over her every time she sees him, let alone hears his voice.

"I'm working on it this very moment, Mr Chandler," Dan says. Elin has never seen the blacksmith so quiet and courteous.

"That wasn't the question, Dan. The vicar wants to know

when the gate will be hung. He has arranged an event on the lawn the first Sunday of next month and he wants the new gates in position.

"Well, with a bit of luck—"

"No, not luck, Dan. With hard work. A good day to you."

Sunlight floods in through the smithy doorway. Elin leaves enough time for the official to get out of sight before venturing out herself. She decides to keep her clogs on her feet for the time being to avoid attracting attention. She walks along the road towards the Ceidrych valley and, once out of sight of the houses at Felindre on the common, she takes off her clogs, pushes her hands into them and starts to run. The farm at Tal-y-garn is her first port of call. Ianto is the link there. Ianto is a lad about a year older than her – slim, strong and with a permanent smile. She finds him feeding the pigs in their sty in the farmyard.

"Midnight. The Efail-fach. Under Garn Goch."

"How are you, Elin *fach*? Am I pleased to see you. I haven't seen a soul all day. Everyone's so busy at the moment, aren't they? And you're keeping well, are you?"

"Ianto, I have to go."

"Yes, of course. But tell me now, which route would you think is the best way to take the message round the Ceidrych valley – up to the Garn first and down to Glan Tywi and work your way back, or the other way round?"

"Ianto, you're not supposed to tell me the places you call at!"

"I'm not? Oh yes, I'm not – I know that of course. But everyone knows where your heart is, Elin! You see, Elin *fach*, this is my first time, and I want so hard to make a tidy job of it. It's quite a responsibility, isn't it? But it's fun foo, I have to admit—"

"Ianto, I have to go."

"Where are you off to next, then?"

"Ianto, I can't tell you!"

"Oh yes, quite right. No, these things have to be a secret. We have to think of people's safety. Now, middle of the night, you said, didn't you?"

"No, Ianto, you have to be specific. Time will be tight. Midnight. The Efail-fach. Under Garn Goch."

"Got it, Elin. I'll tell them that you've told me they mustn't be late."

"No, Ianto. No names. None. D'you understand? Certainly don't name me. But don't name people in the Ceidrych valley to each other either. We have to keep names out of it."

"You're quite right, Elin *fach*. The Dragoons are like weeds this summer – they're everywhere. And there are some among us with sly ears. No names, then."

"Very good, Ianto. Now, it's time for you to take the message round."

"Of course, of course. But tell me, Elin – will Llew the blacksmith be Beca again this time?"

"Ianto! No names!"

"Quite right! Quite right!"

Elin sighs and gets going along the field path which will take her straight to Siân at Carregfoelgam.

Chapter 14

At half past eleven that night, Gwyndaf is walking through the Ceidrych valley in the company of Jorjo, Tom and a gang of brawny men in women's clothes.

"How many of us are there?"

"Oh, a good crowd, Gwyndaf!" Jorjo says. "Over fifty, I'd say – and the Llangadog lads are coming along the lower road and the Ffair-fach lads are coming from another direction."

"We must be quite a sight!" Tom says. "The white petticoats and nightdresses – it's as if every woman in the area is sleepwalking!"

"And that they've forgotten to wash before turning in!" Jorjo jokes, looking about him at the whole gang with blackened faces.

Gwyndaf suddenly trips and is saved from falling headlong by Tom, who grabs his arm.

"Are you alright?"

"Yes," Gwyndaf replies. "This is Elin's nightgown. It touches the floor when she wears it – and she's a couple of inches taller than me, isn't she?"

"You'll have to carry your axe in one hand and lift the skirt of the nightgown with the other, like her ladyship in Newton House!" Jorjo says.

"There you go – ve'y refayn'd, just like her ladyship in the big house!" Tom laughs, then says: "I'll tell you one thing – this isn't how the Dragoons march into battle, is it!"

The knot of men around them had laughed at Tom's imitation of a fine lady lifting the edge of her petticoat as she delicately twirled a couple of dance steps on the lawn of Newton House in Dinefwr Park. But the laughter dies away as the vision of the mounted soldiers is conjured up in each imagination.

Then, to break the silence, Gwyndaf says, "Beca looks good on her white pony."

"Doesn't she just!" Jorjo says. "You wouldn't believe the scene in the smithy as she got herself ready. Her head's wrapped up in a turban, which is holding straw in place to look like golden locks. She's got several petticoats on, one on top of the other then a colourful shawl and a garland of flowers round her neck. The finishing touch is a red *diklo*, how you would say – a scarf, worn as a belt, holding everything in place! She looks like a queen! A queen bearing an axe!"

"And isn't Dicw taking it all in his stride?" Gwyndaf says.

"Yes. He's been trimmed with ribbons everywhere – you wouldn't know him. I'll be standing beside him the whole time when they light the torches and sound the horn and fire a shot or two into the air. He'll be quiet enough if I'm there."

The party goes on and joins those on the lower road by the Groesffordd Inn and they travel on, past Geidrych Mill.

"There's some people on the slope to the left here," Tom says. "Can you make them out?"

"That's the path down from Llwyn Du, that is. It'll be the Capel Gwynfe lads coming down from the shoulder of Garn Goch. They look like ghosts!"

The men hear owl hoots and the bark of a dog-fox from the moorland path and then about thirty men from the mountain run down the slope towards them, brandishing cudgels and other weapons and screaming like the Devil's own.

"Are you ready for the Gwynfe Angels?" bellows the leader, decked out in a white petticoat.

"I know whose that rough voice is!" Gwyndaf shouts back. "Deri Ysgubor Wen!"

"Lad, lad – don't let the cat out of the bag!" replies the 'angel'. "Or I'll be shouting that Gwyndaf Tafarn y Wawr is here too!"

"Good to see you, Deri – and Morgan Cwm-cou ... and Elis Bryn-coch!" There is much merriment as the two groups recognise each other, despite the soot and strange clothing.

"Is that axe keen enough?" Morgan asks.

"Where's the whacking to be tonight then, *bois*?" Elis asks.

"Is there enough fire in these here bellies?" asks Deri.

The united crowd surges onward to meet up with a huge army that has already assembled at Efail-fach. A great whoop of greeting goes up as they see Beca on her white pony, ready to lead them through the dark night.

The door of the Efail-fach smithy stands open, and Beca is greeted by the dancing flames of the forge.

"Light the torches, my children!" she shouts.

"We need enough light for dark deeds!" says Morgan as he lights his torch from the flames in the smithy.

"The flames of hell for the toll-house!" Elis says.

"*Jiw, jiw* – keep that thing away from my petticoat, *crwt*!"

131

Deri says. "There'll be hell to pay if I go home with burn holes in my missus' petticoat!"

Once the torches are alight and the army has sorted itself out into a procession, Beca explains the next step.

"Forward, my children! I wish for a journey to Llandeilo without let or hindrance!"

The men pass Tŷ-gwyn-bach and Llwyn-maen-du Isaf. A meander of the river Tywi brings it close to the road on that side of the valley. The crowd marches boisterously, sounding the horn and firing their guns, and all the while the timeless, quiet Tywi and the silent meadows lie to their right. It is as if there is no one else on the face of the earth except for Rebecca and her Daughters.

"So, onwards to the Pontbren Araeth Gate!" cries Morgan.

"Couldn't be better! A quarter moon – just enough to see what we're hitting!" cries Elis.

"The Araeth river sings in the dingle – we'll have a tune to toil to, *bois*!" Deri says.

"Come on, mate. More work and less romanticising!" says Morgan.

Some of the Daughters arrive at the gate with much baying and howling. Beca on her pony comes up behind them and shouts, in a loud, strong voice: "My Daughters! Why do you not move forward? We need to go to Llandeilo, if you remember."

Then one of the Daughters beside the gate shouts: "We can't go forward, Mother! There is something across the road!"

Rebecca grows impatient. "Make way! Let me see what's

the matter! Shoo, shoo, get out of the way!"

The Daughters then chorus: "What is it, Mother? There shouldn't be anything stopping an old woman like you from getting to her destination!"

"I can't understand it, my Daughters," Beca says. "I'm so old, my Daughters. My eyes grow dim. Wait a moment for me to make this out."

Rebecca leans over from her saddle and strikes the wood of the gate with her axe.

"Oooh! It has a hollow sound! I think it's a dead tree that's fallen across the road. Did we have a storm yesterday, my Daughters?"

"No we didn't, Mother," the Daughters reply.

Rebecca goes over and taps the post, the lock and the latch of the gate.

"No, it's not a tree but a gate! There's a chain on the gate and it's locked! Gates are for keeping animals in their place, aren't they, my Daughters?"

"Yes!"

"And we're not animals, are we, my Daughters?"

"No!"

"Someone's made an error, my Daughters. What shall we do, then?"

"We'll break the gate, Mother!"

The sound of saws and axes and sledgehammers doing their work shatters the night air.

In five minutes, the gate is in pieces. The smallest chips are gathered together and set alight with the torches. Then those equipped with a crowbar and sledgehammer get to work on the gateposts. The sound of iron hitting iron. Sparks fly. And then it's all over.

"Hey, Dan, there's probably some good bits of iron here for the forge!" Gwyndaf laughs and turns towards Dan Dowlais.

"No need to tell me, mate – I've already got half a sackful. The gate-hooks and chain are just by your feet – kick them over here, would you?"

After the roadway has been cleared, Beca on her pony stands before the door of Bridge House and calls on the toll-keeper to come out.

"The flames are rather close to the roof!" Beca says. "Come on out quietly, and no harm will come to you."

Nothing happens for a while. The crowd falls silent ...

Then the door opens and the toll-keeper emerges with his head bowed, looking wretched. He faces the Daughters of Rebecca barefoot and in his nightshirt.

"This is a warning from Beca and her Daughters," says the voice mounted on the pony. "On pain of being punished far worse than tonight, you will never again be a gatekeeper, demanding money from the common country folk who use this road. Never again, d'you understand?"

The crowd roars as if for his blood, and brandish their weapons skyward.

"Never again – what is your reply?" Beca demands.

The toll-keeper shakes his head as if to say he will never again do such a thing. After another cheer from the Daughters, the toll-keeper goes back inside the house.

"Are we letting the fox go back to his den?" Morgan asks.

"Are we leaving the Trust's house and its roof intact?" Elis asks.

"Are we going on to smash another gate?" Deri asks.

"Home, away home, you wild mountain boys!" Gwyndaf says. "This is enough for one night! "

* * *

The following morning, as she goes into her brother's bedroom, Elin looks at his dark hair as he lies in a deep sleep. She opens the curtains. A groan emerges from the bed. She sees that Gwyndaf has turned his back towards the window and has buried his head under the bedclothes.

She walks round to the other side of the bed. She pulls the bedclothes down a little so her brother's face comes back into view. Deep grooves appear on his forehead as he tries to squeeze his eyes shut.

"I've brought you a bowl of bread and buttermilk, Gwyndaf. It's warm. You must be starving. I've but a spoonful of honey in with it, for you to get some strength back."

She holds the bowl under her brother's nose for a long while. Gradually, Gwyndaf breathes more easily and the frown slackens. He squints at his sister.

"Oh, it's late, Gwyndaf. You've been asleep for hours. It's almost dinner time ..."

Gwyndaf straightens up and starts to rub his eyes. He's just about to throw the bedclothes off and get up.

"No, no!" Elin laughs. "I'm only pulling your leg. It's not that late. Now, have a bit of this bread and buttermilk with honey."

Gwyndaf has no sooner put the first spoonful in his mouth than Elin asks her first question. She doesn't let up until she's extracted every last detail about the previous night from her brother.

* * *

"And that's the whole story?"

"Yes, I'd better get up now ..."

"No, you're alright for another two hours. Mam and Dad aren't up yet!"

"What! You woke me up early just to find out what happened?"

"What happened is important to me, Gwyndaf. I was on tenterhooks all last night, thinking about you. I almost ran up to the summit of Garn Goch to see if I could spot the procession."

"Yes, fair play to you, Elin. It wouldn't have been such a good night without the work you put in."

Elin looks at her brother tenderly for a minute, without saying a word.

"Why the puppy-eyes, Elin? What's the matter now?"

"You."

"What have I done now?"

"If you had woken me up too early – two hours before it was time to get up! – and then admitted as much, I'd have jumped out of bed, half-throttled you against the wall and then carried you outside and stuck your head in the spring. But what do you do? Smile sweetly and say, 'Fair play to you,

Elin'!" It is Gwyndaf's turn to be quiet now. Elin sees the gentleness in his eyes. "Isn't it odd that we're so different, Gwyndaf. To think that we're brother and sister – twins, at that."

"It's nature, isn't it, Elin. We have two grandmothers and two grandfathers, so there's bound to be an amazing mix in us. You're taller than me; I'm shorter and stockier – I tripped over in your nightgown last night! But it's the same in every family. Take ... Eleri and Siôn, Glan Sawdde. Brother and sister – neither of them married – she's got a face like a wet Wednesday all day, every day, grumpy and miserable with everyone, and he's like a ray of sunshine all day, every day – and at night too. The only thing that's important to her is her, but he's part of the community. He was with us last night!"

"Yes, but we're twins ..."

"Watcyn Harries, the grocer in Llandeilo, has twins. You can pull the leg of one and he's full of fun, but the other one's too important for you to tease and have a bit of a laugh with, and he's dozy with it. No, I don't think we're as different as all that, Elin."

"You've got dark hair, like a Welsh Black bull, but I've got hair as yellow as gorse ..."

"I've got Mam's hair and you take after Mam-gu, Dad's mother, don't you? That's what they say."

"Do you remember her, Gwyndaf? Nerys, wasn't it?"

"Of course I do, we were nine when she died, I remember her well ..."

"Do you remember the colour of her hair, then?"

"Well, I remember her with white hair – but then again she

was old by then. Dad's got a touch of blond in his hair, though, hasn't he."

"Yes, my memories of her are with white hair too ... Do you have dreams, Gwyndaf?"

"Dreams ...? No, I don't think so – well, maybe I do but I can't remember them when I wake up. There's always other things need doing, aren't there, once you're out of bed."

"I have amazing dreams ... And sometimes they stay with me all day."

"Did you dream last night?"

"No. But then I didn't sleep much either."

"There you go then – that's the answer. Don't sleep. You won't dream then!"

* * *

Her mother is up and has finished clearing up in the pub by the time Elin goes back downstairs.

"What time did he get home last night?"

"I don't know," Elin says, and as she says it her thoughts go back to Nest Morgan, Pont Goch Cottage.

"No good will come of rising up against authority. Those prison ships are full of people who thought they were too clever to be caught."

Elin goes out into the yard. She sees that her father is backing the horse between the shafts of the cart.

"And where do you get to go today, Seren, and it being Sunday and all?"

"Well, yes, it is 'Sunday and all'," says Brython Rees. "And so it'd be just as well if we stopped this nonsense and make peace, don't you think, Elin? And I'll tell you straight what's going on. Himself, Mr Chandler, wants us to move some tables out of the vestry and into the vicarage coach house so that the servants can clean and paint them, ready for the event in the garden in August."

"Mr Chandler's giving you quite a bit of work, isn't he, Dad?"

"How can I refuse Mr C? The church own this pub. We're only tenants – and tenants can never show their teeth, can they? If he wants me and the cart, I go. But he wants me to take a barrel down to the event and all – so that'll mean more money coming to us to pay the rent to the church. There's going to be a refreshment tent in the garden, you see."

"Sunday, August the sixth. The vicar's son is twenty-one—"

"So, he's another one that's living on the parish, is he, Dad?" says Elin, her voice barbed. She turns on her heel and heads for the path up the slope.

Chapter 15

When Elin reaches the hill leading up to Coed yr Arlwydd, she becomes aware that there is something strange about the atmosphere of the common. As she approaches the clearing, she sees four enormous horses tethered by their reins to a low branch. Dragoons, she thinks. She is in two minds about pressing on towards the Lee family but just at that moment one of the Dragoons comes into view between the trees and looks threateningly at her.

Too late now to turn back, she thinks. She tries to walk nonchalantly into the clearing and greets Jorjo, Mari Lee and the rest of the family cheerfully. All the while, her mind is racing. What can I give as an excuse for the visit? Why am I here at this time in the morning? She quickly hits on a brainwave.

"Mari Lee, I've come for you to tell my fortune! I gave you a shilling last week, didn't I, and you told me to go home and dream for three nights. Well, here I am."

"Come close, Elin *fach*," Mari says, catching on immediately. "I'll take a look at your palm and listen to your dreams now, just as soon as these gentlemen have finished their visit. Come and sit by my side and put your hand in my lap here."

"What on earth! You will not speak that foreign tongue in front of me!"

"He his Capten off da Dragoons," Jorjo says, with a polite smile, gesturing to the man with his open hand. He knows from long experience how to behave courteously and pleasantly while maintaining his dignity. He continues, in Welsh, "They've come from Llan'dyfri today, you see. They haven't seen Dicw, mind."

"Is that the native lingo they're speaking, Taffy?" the captain asks the smallest of the three Dragoons. "You can speak it, can't you?"

"Yes," he replies. "It is Anglesey I am from – and no, it's not Welsh what they speak. It's gyppo language I'm thinking. I can't know a word of it."

"She ... wants fortune," says Mari Lee, pointing at Elin and showing her hand.

"Where was she last night?" The captain approaches Elin and shouts in her face: "Where were you last night?"

Elin shakes her head and shows her hand. In Welsh, she says to Mari Lee, "Tell him that Dad has borrowed Dicw and that he's moving stuff by the church, if he asks."

"What she's saying, the stupid girl? What was that about 'Dacw'?" the captain asks.

"She ... wants ... name of love," says Mari Lee in a passionately romantic voice. "See ... beautiful song ... of love." She holds her hand over her heart and starts singing: "*Dacw 'nghariad i lawr yn y berllan, dwylo brwnt fel gwaelod sosban.*"

The captain waves his hand to indicate that he's lost patience with her.

"So you did not hear anything last night?" he asks, turning to Jorjo.

Jorjo shakes his head, puts his hands together, and leans his head sideways onto his hands to mime sleep.

"Yes, yes. And where's your horse?"

"*Dacw nghariad yn golchi'i ddwylo, coch a gwyn yw'r lliwiau arno,*" Elin sings, as if she's so in love she's totally lost her wits, but all the while following Mari's lead in substituting words in the well-known song.

"Man borrow ..." says Jorjo, taking some money out of his pocket. "Good money ... good. Down in church ..."

The captain looks dubiously at Jorjo, and then in the direction Jorjo is pointing.

"Are you saying that you have lent your horse for a fee and that it's being used at the church in the village?"

Jorjo smiles and claps his hands. The others join in the applause.

"And what colour is this horse of yours? Colour ...? What colour is it?" The captain points at his black riding boots and puts on a questioning face.

Jorjo shakes his head. He remembers Elin's made-up words: *Coch a gwyn yw'r lliwie arno* – red and white.

The captain points at the white stripes on his military uniform and makes a questioning face again.

Jorjo makes a big show of waving his arms about to show that, once more, the captain hasn't chosen the right colour. Then he runs towards the tent and holds up a corner of the canvas, which is a russet colour – he points at that. He goes over then to Elin's blouse and points at the white stripes in the fabric.

"Right, so you have a chestnut and white horse. Proper

gyppo horse by the sound of it. We're wasting our time here, just as we're doing everywhere else. Back to the village!"

The captain walks imperiously through the clearing with two of the other Dragoons right behind him. The one who he'd called 'Taffy' is trailing slightly behind.

He turns so his back is towards his fellow soldiers and in a low voice aimed at Elin, says, in his northern Welsh: "If we see a chestnut and white horse by the church, we'll know that it's the borrowed horse, won't we, *hogan*?"

He winks before turning and following the other soldiers. They all remain in the clearing, shocked and speechless for a minute.

Mari Lee has held Elin's hand in her lap throughout this incident. After the sound of the horses has disappeared, she looks at her hand and asks: "Do you want me to look into the future, Elin?"

After a moment's hesitation, Elin withdraws her hand.

"What will be, will be, Mari Lee."

"Yes," she replies, "but we can also look back on what has happened, you know."

"No, I don't have much interest in doing that either," Elin says.

* * *

Well before half past nine the following Thursday evening, the burial ground of the chapel in Cwmifor is pretty full. Although she is not yet eighteen, so not old enough to attend a Rebecca meeting, Elin has had permission from Llew the blacksmith to be there in case a message needs to be run somewhere quickly. She sees that Ianto Tal-y-garn is there, as are several others she recognises as runners. None of them pays her any attention, but when Ianto passes her, he flicks up the collar of his jacket to give her a sneaky wink as he goes by. As if no one would notice him!

"How many people are here?" she asks Llew, when she bumps into him.

"Between three and four hundred. It's a good crowd. All roads lead to this little valley tonight."

"Hey, Llew," says one of the men at the entrance, coming towards them, "there's some English bloke at the gate. He wants to come to the meeting but the lads guarding the gate feel he shouldn't be here. This is a meeting for us. But he's insistent – and the lad who's with him is too."

"Who are they?" Llew asks.

"Come over to see them."

Llew beckons to Elin to come with him. As they approach the gate, she sees it's Thomas Foster and Dylan Lloyd who are trying to gain entry to the meeting.

"Listen, *bois*," says Llew to the stewards, "this gentleman's come all the way here from London. He's gathering stories about the roots of the problems that are behind what the Daughters of Rebecca are doing."

"Painting us as the devils to the grand people, that's what you're saying, is it?" says a young man with wild eyes.

"No. He writes reports for *The Times*, the paper that important people in London take notice of."

"But that's a paper in English, isn't it?" says another. "How can he touch the hearts of the Welsh people – in English?"

Dylan Lloyd steps forward to the group discussing this in Welsh, and adds, in their common language: "I'm guiding him round the countryside. He's been speaking with hundreds of people – ordinary people like you. I try and convey the views of Welsh people to him, in his own language."

"But they twist our words, just like the lawyers in the courts," says the lad with wild eyes. "The meaning they come out with is different to our meaning."

"Thomas Foster doesn't put a slant on the truth. He respects facts," Llew says.

"Have you read his reports, Llew?"

"I do that," says Dylan immediately. "He asks me if his words are fair before he sends them off to London. Many of the newspapers are taking notice of the destruction and unrest here. 'Outrage,' they say. 'We have to restore order,' they say. They praise the government for sending two thousand soldiers here. They run down the common people just for being Welsh. They're not prepared to listen to the complaints nor understand the causes behind these actions. They're not prepared to play fair or change the laws they foist on us from London. But Thomas Foster is giving voice to your protests, he's describing the poverty he's seeing, he's showing how the tolls and the tithes and the cost of food and the cost of carrying goods is destroying lives and sending families to the workhouse. The reason he's come here tonight is to listen to more of your stories, to meet more ordinary folk so he can send more evidence to the paper in London. Down here in the Tywi valley, your weapons are the axe and the sledgehammer. But he can add to them his weapons: words and descriptions and the stories he's been told by people. And in the end, that's what's going to get things changed for the better."

"I couldn't have said it better myself!" says Llew. "Are you prepared to let them into the graveyard now, *bois*?"

"Well, alright, then," admits the lad with wild eyes. "But he must stay close to the wall, out of the way."

"And no interrupting and asking for the meeting to be held in English!" says another.

"I'll be translating every word," promises Dylan.

"Yeah, well, you'd better do that quietly too."

The gate is opened and the two journalists take their place among the gravestones.

"I'm sure I should be grateful that there's no welcome for me in a graveyard!" says Dylan to Elin.

"Nervous of strangers, that's all it is," Elin says.

"We came through the river on the Godre Garreg cart," says the blacksmith. "You know the name of the ford – Rhyd-y-Saeson. On the other side there's a wooded hillside and its name is Allt-y-Saeson. They've been sending soldiers from London to try and keep us in our place for centuries, you see. The land still remembers that."

Jac from the Plough Inn comes over to tell Llew that the minister from the new chapel has been chosen to chair the meeting.

"There's a good chance that something's going to happen here before long," adds the innkeeper. "I'm not keen on big gatherings like this. I see them like a cart stuck in the mud –

can't go back and can't go forwards."

A boy about the same age as Elin charges through the crowd.

"Jac?" he says, dispensing with formalities.

One of the runners, thinks Elin. She feels a pride swelling inside to be face to face with one of the others who share the same task as she does. Despite not knowing him, or even his name, she feels a kind of connection with the lad.

"Message from Iori ..."

"Yes? Where have they gone tonight?"

"Brechfa."

"Thank you, lad. You do your disappearing act now."

The boy turns and heads for the gate.

The innkeeper moves close to Llew and Elin hears him whisper: "The Llan'dyfri Dragoons have gone out towards Cil-y-cwm. The Llandeilo Dragoons have made for Brechfa. The coast is clear for you in Llangadog tonight."

The blacksmith nods. The innkeeper goes on to another knot of people, but not before saying: "We have to keep the pressure up, Llew. There might be stories of poverty and injustice in the paper, but force and flame – that's what'll make the bigwigs in London stir themselves into doing something about the situation. I don't think many of them understand any other language."

Llew and Elin watched the innkeeper walk from group to group. He exchanges pleasantries, and shares a joke with one or two, but at the same time his track through the crowd is purposeful as he makes his way to the next person to whom he needs to pass on the important message.

"It'll be in Llangadog tonight, Elin," the blacksmith says. "Tonight. Midnight. Pont ar Frân. Got it? Three trees, three arches, three rivers. Remember?"

Elin nods.

"Follow the wall of the graveyard between the headstones this way. Tell everyone you know and tell them to share the message – but only with those that they know. I'll go this way round the graveyard and over to the trees above the stream. I'll see you later."

After she has given the message to at least half a dozen men from the Llangadog area, Elin turns to see how the smith is doing. Under one of the trees above the stream she sees that he's talking to the man in the black cravat. She's not surprised to see him there. But then she sees him put his hand into the inside pocket of his coat and draw out a roll of paper. She sees him give the roll to Llew.

Just then the meeting starts. The minister gives a long account, summarising the situation of the county's families and communities. Speaker after speaker gets to his feet to share his concerns and declare his opposition to the regime and laws that are starving them.

Eventually it is too dark for the meeting to continue in the open air.

"Come into the schoolhouse behind the chapel," the minister offers.

Hundreds squash into the room. In the crush by the door, Elin finds herself beside Jorjo and Tom, who exchange a few words with her.

"Mind your pockets," comes a voice beside them. Elin

turns to see the lad with the wild eyes who was beside the gate before the meeting began. "There are gypsies among us."

"Hey! That's enough of that! There's no place for hateful words here!" says Elin, the heat of her temper giving confidence to her words. "What you just said is bare-faced lies and complete bigotry! I know these people. They're good friends. You're painting them all with the same brush. You ignorant pig!"

"Alright, alright! No need to fly off the handle, *croten*," he replies. "Only a bit of leg-pulling. It was a joke. Don't you think they can take a joke, eh? Don't they have a sense of humour?"

"What you said wasn't funny," Elin says tartly. "And when was the last time you laughed at yourself, eh? You should treat others as you'd wish to be treated yourself."

Inside the schoolhouse, the meeting passes a number of proposals. To call for an investigation into the worries weighing on the common people. Tax reductions were called for. That there should be an army of principles to support the weak, rather than an army of soldiers to oppress them. There were calls to do away with gates on those small country roads that are maintained by people of the parish, and even that coal, limestone and produce be carried toll-free on the highways. That the Poor Law be amended and that taxes and tithes to the church be abolished.

A roar of approval rises from the crowd when the proposals are read aloud to the audience to round off the meeting. Once the meeting is over, the crowd disperses into the darkness. But the night's work isn't over for quite a few of them.

Elin sticks close by Llew's side to get back to the farmer's cart that is to take them back to Llangadog. At the graveyard gate they come across the two journalists again.

"That was a very well organised and orderly meeting," Dylan Lloyd tells them. "It's difficult to see how the authorities can ignore the message from the community leaders. That's what tonight was. And how do they think their latest move to try and settle the dispute will work against a crowd in a graveyard and a chapel schoolhouse?"

"What move is that then? What have they done now?" asks the blacksmith.

"Didn't you hear? Thomas Foster got hold of the story and it appeared in the paper yesterday under his name. Last Sunday, on the orders of the government, four cannons that fire six-pound cannonballs, and two big ones that can fire twelve-pounders, were prepared to be sent from Woolwich. They came by train to Bristol and they've arrived in Carmarthen now."

"Good grief! Cannons, you say!" says Llew. "They can't catch Beca and her Daughters with the fastest horses in the army. How on earth do they think they'll catch them with cannons?"

"But it sounds like they're preparing for a war against us," Elin says.

"What are they going to do with the cannons, then?" asks the blacksmith. "Are they planning to smash all the county's chapels or something?"

Dylan laughs, but then swallows his laughter. He leans in closer to them and says in a low voice, "One experience

Thomas Foster would very much like to witness is to see an attack on a toll-gate by Rebecca and her Daughters. That would give him the authenticity to say exactly what's happening. He can do justice to the whole drama of the night. It would be an eye-opener for the people in London. Do you think there's any chance he could see that?"

"Nothing much is going on at the moment," Llew says without batting an eyelid. "We've got quite a quiet period ahead of us for a while, as I understand it. That's what I've heard, in any case. I'm not really involved in these things."

The journalist from the *Journal* nods.

"Could we perhaps arrange something, then?"

"Perhaps."

The blacksmith and Elin continue down the road in Cwmifor. Once the crowd has thinned out, Llew chuckles to himself.

"What's tickled you now?" Elin asks.

"Yes, just a quiet night ahead of us tonight. Only going home, dressing up like a woman and smashing up a gate!"

* * *

Very early the next morning, Elin is once again in her brother's bedroom asking about the previous night's goings on. By now Gwyndaf knows he can't keep her out until she's had the whole story and in his head he's already prepared an account with no detail omitted.

"There was more of a crowd this time than the last. So many had gathered beside Pont ar Frân and the mill that it was difficult to get the procession organised. But we got going eventually – turned towards the village first, but we cut across by Dolau-bach, turned left and then crossed Nant Dyrfal and onward to the gate at Waun-Ystrad-Feurig. The gatekeeper was a real cocky one – he thought he could tell anyone and everyone what was what. The gate was smashed and his roof set alight. The toll-house windows were smashed too and the crowd carried the little turkey-cock out, even though his wife begged for forgiveness on his behalf. Beca left them to look for another home and warned them to never work as toll-keepers ever again. Then, we went back to the village and attacked the doors and windows of the church vestry."

"The church vestry? Why?"

"That's where they keep the account books for the church tithes and taxes. Two big holes were made in the door."

"Oh, himself, Chandler, will be overjoyed today!"

"He'll not be happy with the warning that was nailed to the door, either."

Chapter 16

After hearing the rest of her brother's story, Elin felt the urge to go down to Llangadog to see if the warning on the vestry door was still there. She couldn't explain it. She just had to read it.

It doesn't take her long to run down through the fields. She puts her clogs back on and walks, past the pubs in the square, towards the church. It is still early and there is no one about except those who have to go to work at that time.

As she gets closer to the vestry, she can see two holes in the door, like two dark eyes. They look like the eye sockets in a skull, she thinks. How easy it would have been for Rebecca and her Daughters to enter the building last night and burn the account books, she thinks. Her heart starts racing when she sees that the piece of paper is still there, still nailed to the wood between the two holes in the door.

She walks cautiously towards it. She is drawn to it. But there is something holding her back too. The message is written in a confident hand. Someone who is used to writing has done it. She stands before the door and starts to read.

Llangadog,
20th July 1843

Richard Chandler, I have received plaints from the parishioners you have been burdening with church tithes and taxes. It is a dreadful thing to be a servant of the church and to make paupers of the parishioners, causing them to be turned out of their homes and sent straight to the Poorhouse. You behave barbarically – woe! woe! And indeed woe!

The warning is referring to Edryd and Nest Morgan, thinks Elin. Their fate needs to be broadcast to all and sundry. She keeps reading.

My Daughters and I have lately made diligent enquiries, and amongst other things we hear of you is the imputation that you are dishonest with the monies you exact under the pretext that the church tax is spent on the costs of church services and is distributed amongst the paupers of the parish ...

That's what everyone in the parish says, thinks Elin. Squeezing money out of the people and then the money is kept by the vicar and his officials. Who is paying for the swanky new gates at the vicarage? Who is paying for the big party for the vicar's son, come to that? This is a good letter, she says to herself. She turns back to it and reads on.

In addition to this heinous behaviour, three instances have been brought to my attention by my Daughters in this parish where advantage was taken of young maidens and of a woman of the neighbourhood. Twenty years ago, you took advantage on more than one occasion of a young virgin who had neither strength nor authority to demur. When she discovered that she was with child, you sent her to the Poorhouse. There her son was born and there he lived without a penny of subsistence from you. He was obliged to join Her Majesty's navy as a cabin boy ...

Elin's hand flies to her mouth in shock. That is a serious accusation to make in public, she thinks. But it must be true. Elin herself has heard of such incidents in local grand houses, where there are several maids. The odd farm, too. But by a church official! Snake-eyes becomes yet more loathsome in her mind.

Eighteen years ago, the same thing occurred, but on this occasion to a grown woman who could not defend herself because you had bound her arms behind her in the wood ...

Things went from bad to worse, Elin tells herself. No one had ventured to stand up publicly against the old goat before. But things had changed.

Then, sixteen years ago, after you had ruined one of the vicarage maidservants by defilement, she passed away whilst giving birth. Vile attacks on women turned into a case of murder ...

Murder! Chandler was a murderer on top of everything else! And then she read the warning in the final paragraph:

You will transfer your small fortune, bled from your parishioners, to the children of the Poorhouse and then you will leave the area.

You know that I demolish and destroy toll-gates and toll-houses. If you do not obey my command, you will be reduced to splinters, like the toll-gates, when I come across you, because I stand against all manner of oppression.

Yours,
Rebecca and her Daughters

Elin feels weak by the time she reaches the end of the warning on the door. She knows that Rebecca has issued such warnings to other people too. She had heard of a warning being given to a farmer who had taken possession of a farm after another family had been turned off it. Several landowners had had warnings. But the accusations here were a matter for the law ...

"Read it to me, Elin."

Elin turns to face Mari Lee. She had been so lost in thought, she hadn't heard her footsteps coming down the street.

"I know it's disgusting," the woman says. "I heard about this from Jorjo. But I need to hear it. Read it."

Elin hears a note of ferocity in Mari Lee's voice. Her dark eyes are blazing. Elin obeys, even though some of the words stick in her throat. The man makes her want to vomit. When she reaches the final paragraph, she hears Mari Lee let out a deep sigh behind her.

"At last, it's been said! It's public, after all these years. Thank goodness we have Beca now ... He's pure evil!"

"What d'you think'll happen after this then, Mari Lee?"

"Oh, the law won't want to know, I can tell you that now! But the truth stands, my dear. Come on, I've got one more thing to do before getting out of this village."

Elin follows the gypsy without a word.

The pair walk down Church Street and into Vicarage Road. Then the woman stands, with Elin behind her, in front of the door to one of the posh houses. At every window at the front of the house the curtains are closed, although there's a light to be seen at the back, where the maidservants are at their work. Elin doesn't dare utter a word. Suddenly, Mari Lee turns and crosses the road to pick up a hefty piece of red sandstone from the front wall of Cwrt y Plas farm. She walks quickly back to the posh house and then, before Elin can say or do anything, she throws the stone through the window beside the door. The crash echoes down the street. The summer morning's peace is shattered. One minute there's no one in the street, the next, doors are opening and heads are protruding from windows. Elin hears the window above their heads opening. She looks up to see that Richard Chandler has partly opened a curtain and is leaning out of the window in his dressing gown. He is on the point of opening his mouth to shout, but Elin sees that he's quickly realised that it's Mari Lee standing in front of his house.

The gypsy stands defiantly, looking up at him, her fingers balled into fists and those fists on her hips. She is challenging him to say something.

The church official withdraws his head and whips the curtain closed.

Before Elin has a chance to say anything, the side door opens and a short, round woman wearing a white apron and cap emerges. It is Heddwenna the cook. She walks like a corgi, her shoulders and backside rolling, and her meaty arms are flailing.

"What are you doing you, you no good gyppo, you?" she roars at Mari Lee. "Have you lost your mind? Breaking the window of a respectable gentleman here in the village. Have you no fear of the law or the Lord? You're going straight to gaol, and good riddance to you!"

Mari Lee doesn't even look at her.

"Catrin!" Chandler's cook has turned to shout towards the back door.

"Catrin!"

The under-housemaid runs out of the house.

"Go and fetch a brush and dustpan!"

She runs back into the house and runs out once more, carrying them.

"There's glass on the ground under this window, thanks to the handiwork of this wildcat from the woods! Sweep it up. Then go into the study and clear up the mess in there. I'm going to have a word with Mr Chandler to see when the law will be able to come to take her away."

Mari Lee stands her ground without a word.

By now the odd head sticking out of a door has grown to be knots of people here and there. Villagers from other streets are arriving. Some are pointing towards the vestry and the night's work. It's clear that the message and warning on the paper nailed to the door is a talking point.

After scooping up the largest pieces of glass into her dustpan, Catrin takes them round the back of the house.

No one comes near Mari Lee and she doesn't say a word to Elin either. Elin starts thinking, how long she can stay like this in the street, with me standing between her and those people whispering amongst themselves? She herself has had nothing to do with breaking the window, after all.

From where Elin is standing, she can see the study door opening and Catrin entering the room with her brush and dustpan. Mari Lee goes forward until she is right beside the hole in the window.

"Give me that rock that's on the table – I'll go and put in back on the wall."

Catrin looks nervously at her.

"How does he treat you, Catrin *fach*? Does he push up against you when he passes you on the stairs, and you've got your arms full? And what does he do then? Does he lean over you when you're bent over laying the fire in his study? Do you have to take him a cup of tea when he's in bed, or a glass of port late at night, maybe ...?"

Catrin's head bows lower with each question.

"Now, pass that rock back to me so I can help you a bit."

Slowly, the under-housemaid puts the dustpan and brush down. She turns to the table and lifts the rock. Without making eye contact, she passes the rock to Mari Lee through the hole in the window.

"Thank you, my dear. I hope you get a better position than the one here before long."

Mari Lee raises the rock above her head and hurls it through another window, on the other side of the imposing front door. A groan of shock and surprise rises from the watching crowd. She turns to her audience in the street and holds her head high.

"The stone can speak. Listen to the stone."

Then she turns towards the vicarage and starts walking.

Elin hears the voices in the street, louder now.

"Where's she going?"

"Oh! Is she going to do the same thing to the vicar?"

"I'll tell you one thing, Mr Chandler's afraid of her!"

Elin glances up at the bedroom curtains again. She sees them move slightly. He's watching, she thinks.

She turns and runs after Mari Lee. What is she going to do next? Has the vicar mistreated someone too?

But the gypsy walks past the vicarage. She walks quickly

on, past the next field and then follows the footpath that will take her back towards Carreg Sawdde Common. She doesn't say a word.

Once they've crossed the footbridge over the little stream, they walk side by side across the common towards the bridge and the toll-house. Mari Lee turns her head towards Elin.

"I need to have a word with the blacksmith. On my own. Didn't you mention a while back that you'd been playing running with the children from the toll-house? You go on to them. Teach them to run fast, especially the girls."

She turns away, leaving Elin standing there as she strides off towards the smithy.

Chapter 17

Elin walks home, rather than running. Part of the notice on the vestry door keeps circling round her head. How did Rebecca know all these stories but she herself had never heard of any of them? And how could she explain what Mari Lee had done?

She suddenly remembers where she'd seen the paper on the vestry door before. In the graveyard at Cwmifor! She recalls seeing the roll of paper being transferred from the pocket of the man in the black cravat to Llew the blacksmith's hands. That thought slows her pace, and makes her think deeper.

When she reaches Tafarn y Wawr, he mother is racing from room to room, trying to do everything at once.

"Where've you been, *croten*? Your tasks are calling. There's masses to do today."

"What's happening?" Elin asks.

"Don't you remember what I told you the other day? Rhys Prydderch the drover arrives today."

"Is it time for him to come already?"

"Now, go and fetch the white tablecloth from the bottom of the dresser and lay it on the table beside the window in the little room at the front. That's his favourite spot – he can eat his meal and enjoy a little tipple and look out over the field and see his sheep."

Every year, Rhys Prydderch is the first of the drovers to call at Tafarn y Wawr at the start of the new season. At the end of the summer, he and his stockmen move the sheep down from the hills above the Tywi valley to graze on the aftermath of the hay harvest in the Honddu, Wye and Usk valleys and farmland of eastern Wales before they go to the markets in London in the autumn.

"Where's Gwyndaf?"

"Oh, he was late getting up! It was a job winkling him out of his bed today. He and his father have gone to fix up a new gate on the Cae Bach field. Rhys Prydderch's sheep need a secure boundary or they'll get out."

"Oh, he can erect gates as well as knock them down, can he?"

"That's enough loose talk! Those matters shouldn't be discussed in this house, *croten*. Some things are best not said. Best to keep quiet."

This is on Elin's mind as she sets the table. Why do people keep quiet about some things. Fear, she decides in the end. People lived in fear. But Beca had opened the door. There was no need to fear everything, as before.

"We need to prepare lamb for supper tonight." Tegwen Rees bustles into the room and reviews Elin's handiwork with the eye of a hawk. She straightens the tablecloth a fraction. She polishes the cutlery to an even higher shine with her apron. She goes to the window and examines it.

"You can clean the window next. And you need to dust the shelf of the small dresser. Come into the kitchen then – we'll get started on the supper so it can be slow-roasted. That's the way the drovers want it."

Later, in the kitchen, Elin wants to raise the matter of the notice on the vestry door, and Mari Lee's reaction to it, but she doesn't know how to start such a conversation. She and her mother don't find it easy to discuss such things. She decides to dive in at the deep end.

"Mari Lee chucked a stone through Richard Chandler's study window this morning."

"What? Good heavens above!" Tegwen Rees sits down suddenly at the table to catch her breath.

"Are you alright, Mam? And then she did the same thing again ... What's the matter, Mam? You could swear the stone had hit you and not Chandler's window ..."

"And then shall evil be revealed – the truth will out," replies her mother, her thoughts far from the pub kitchen.

"What does that mean, Mam? It's not like Mari Lee, is it? She's usually full of the milk of human kindness. And she never said a word to explain why she did it. She's usually full of stories too."

"And full of secrets."

Elin didn't dare break the long silence that followed her mother's words.

"But it's best to forget some secrets and move on," Tegwen says eventually.

"Mari Lee's not like what a lot of people say about gypsies, is she?"

"People always fear people who are outside their everyday understanding," Tegwen says. "People who are different, people—"

"People who aren't respectable like us, is it? Like church people? Like Richard Chandler …?"

Tegwen Rees stands up as quickly as she'd sat down.

"I'll need blackberries for the drovers' pudding. Go out to the fields to pick some for me. They say there'll be heavy rain at the beginning of the week. They'll be ruined after that. There's plenty now in the hedges."

In collecting her bowlful of blackberries, Elin gets closer to the gap where Gwyndaf and her father are hanging the new gate. She starts chatting with them as she picks the glistening fruit from the brambles.

"Did you read the notice on the vestry door last night, Gwyndaf?"

"Yes. One of the Daughters held up a flaming torch so that everyone who wanted to read it – or was able to read it – had the chance to."

"There must have been a lot of discussion afterwards."

"Everyone was talking non-stop. It was all news to me and to many of the others."

"Had you heard these stories, Dad?" Elin asks.

"What stories are those, then?"

"I already told you while we were out here this morning, Dad …" Gwyndaf says.

"Richard Chandler," Elin says. "Well?"

"I'm not one to listen to gossip. You never know what's the truth and what, lies. Is the weather going to hold or is there more rain in the air?"

"But the stories have been written in black and white

now," Elin says, insisting on going back to the same topic.

"I don't know. There's a bit of fog over the Black Mountain, don't you think?"

"But what do you believe, Dad?"

"It's difficult to tell, this time of year – we're on the cusp of the season, aren't we?"

"Dad, you're changing the subject! I saw the same thing with my own eyes this morning," Elin says. "It'll be big news by tonight, bound to be, but I was there."

"What did you see, Elin?" asks Gwyndaf, pleased that for once it's he who is asking the questions rather than the other way around.

Elin tells him the tale of the events in Vicarage Street.

"What do you make of that, then?" she asks them both, once she's finished.

"Tom and Jorjo were with us last night and they heard what was on the notice," Gwyndaf says. "But does Anna know about it?"

"She wasn't there this morning, if that's what you mean."

"If Mari Lee's back in Coed yr Arlwydd, Anna will know," Gwyndaf says ruminatively. They share everything. They're a family with no secrets between themselves."

"I've noticed that," Elin says. "They understand each other because they tell the truth to each other."

"And any fallings out don't last long," Gwyndaf says.

"This gate opens easily now," Brython Rees says, wiggling it back and forth and then pushing it against the opposite post. "Tie a loop of rope to hold it firm to the post, Gwyndaf. Not even Rhys Prydderch's sheep will be able to escape now –

although, having said that, some of them can jump like goats."

"It'll be good to have animals in the fields again," Gwyndaf says. "How long will they be here for?"

"Rhys is bringing about fifty over from the hills down Castell Cennen way today. Then they need to fetch about another forty from Capel Gwynfe tomorrow, and a similar number from Llanddeusant the day after, and then they'll be heading over to Brecon."

"On mountain tracks," Gwyndaf says, looking over towards the Black Mountain.

"Free from all tolls and in their own time!" Elin says. "I reckon I'd like to be a drover."

"It's no job for a woman," says her father.

"Things could change," Elin says. "Boundaries don't stay in the same place for long."

"I'm going to the cellar. I need to tap a barrel for tonight," says her father. "Some of the local farmers are bound to come over tonight to hear what news the drovers bring."

"Gossip, don't you mean, Dad?" Elin asks.

"No, discussing market prices. How the harvest's been in other areas. These things are important. These drovers crisscross the country and they—"

"They chatter worse than a flock of starlings on a dungheap!"

"Are you going to see Mari Lee this afternoon?" Gwyndaf asks his sister, once their father has left them.

"No, Mam will make quite sure that I'm not free today," Elin answers.

"I could go," says Gwyndaf. "But maybe I'd upset the family?"

"*Jiw, jiw*, Gwyn, you know them well enough. And Mari Lee is always open-hearted. If she wants to be left in peace, she'll tell you to go away. Try and slip away this afternoon, then."

Elin works without enough of a break to give the matter any further thought until the drovers arrive. Despite that, a string of words keep returning to unsettle her – *because you had bound her arms behind her in the wood* ... She could see the scene before her very eyes, as if it were real. It's a hellish image, she thinks to herself.

* * *

"Hai-hai-hai, hai-o!"

Towards the end of the afternoon, Elin hears familiar calls coming up the hillside. The drovers have crossed the river Sawdde using one of the hidden fords only they know about, and are walking up the road to the pub. Elin runs out to the yard and opens the new gate for them. Siôn, one of the young stockmen, is walking at the front and the flock is following him; Harri, another young stockman, is shooing them from the back; behind him the old drover, Rhys Prydderch, on his pony, is waving his stick in greeting, and Haden, his red Welsh collie is weaving back and forth behind him. The flock goes into the field without any trouble, with Haden at its heels, left and right.

"How are you, Elin, my dear, the prettiest girl in the

world!" says Rhys Prydderch as he reaches the gate. "Aha! A new gate for the new droving season, is it? What a welcome! Oh, and there's a nice bit of grazing here too. They'll be pretty easy to keep within the hedges for the time being. Where's that brother of yours? He can take my pony to the stable."

The drover dismounts from the pony and hands the reins to the girl.

"He's not here at the moment, Rhys Prydderch. I'll take this dun pony to the stable. He's new, isn't he? I don't think I've seen this one before."

"He came from Tregaron. I bought him in Llanybydder at the start of the summer as I was starting to go round the farms to look at the stock. Cynan. He's a tough pony for the mountains, but there's a streak of temper in him. And he has to have his bellyful of food!"

"Who doesn't!" says Harri. "It's harder going with sheep than with cattle. It's hungry work, this droving."

"Don't you worry, Harri *bach*. You'll have your fill in this pub. You'll sleep like a happy hog in the barn tonight. You take the packs off Cynan now, and follow Elin."

The two stockmen had been on the road, droving, for two years so by now they are familiar with Tafarn y Wawr.

"We're bound to get a welcome in Llangadog. We know that well enough," Harri says. "It's not the same everywhere, though, Elin, believe me. We've got to travel closer to villages and towns once we're over Offa's Dyke. There's no mountains in England where we go, and no free tracks through the uplands. And the taverns are not used to droving men and the extra work we create."

"But you have to admit you look a right mess when you've been following the arses of animals all day!" says Siôn. You're filthy from your head to your clogs, and you stink of shit!"

"When we're getting close to where we're staying, d'you know what those mingy landlords do? They take up the carpets, take down the curtains and put old beer in the jugs!"

"Well, there'll be a cloth on your tables today and the best beer in the jug," says Elin. "But it'd be a good idea to go to the trough in the yard and wash first. I suggest you get it right over your heads!"

The lads laugh.

"Only if you come and wash our backs for us, Elin!" Siôn says.

"You need to wash your mouth out with soap first, *gwboi*!"

Elin takes care of the pony's needs and then shouts up to the stable loft to ask if the lads are all right before going back to the kitchen to help her mother with the meal.

* * *

After the drovers have eaten their fill and enjoyed a couple of tankards of the Plough's beer, there's a very jolly atmosphere in the bar.

The nearby farmers start arriving and there is a lively conversation about the value of stock at market and how many head the drovers will be driving east.

"Are you going on your pony to Capel Gwynfe tomorrow, then, Rhys?" the farmer from Cae-rhyn asks.

"No. I'm going to go round the Llangadog farmers to see

what cattle are available for the droves in the autumn. To see if they're strong enough to walk to England or if they'll fall by the wayside, like the ones I had from you last year!"

"You'll not get better than Llangadog cattle!" says another, fervently.

"I'll see for myself tomorrow. The boys can run to Capel Gwynfe to fetch the sheep," Rhys says.

"Elin here could race them," adds another farmer. "I never saw a faster *croten*!"

"We'll see about that tomorrow, shall we!" Siôn says.

"When are you leaving?" Elin asks.

"With the dawn," Harri says. "After all, it is Tafarn y Wawr – the tavern of the dawn."

"I'll show you the way," says the girl. "You can follow on the best you can."

A wave of laughter engulfs the bar.

Elin goes to the window. Gwyndaf still hasn't returned.

"What's the news around the county?" one of the farmers asks the drovers.

"It's Beca this and Beca that everywhere," says Rhys. "But there are several other things getting people het up too. I've just come from Cwm Cennen. There's a big row over Llandybïe way – the big house has stolen the common land by Hendre Agored and the Gwinau valley, and they're enclosing the village common now."

"Yeah, enclosing Hendre Agored does rather make a mockery of the name, doesn't it?" says another.

"You've still got Carreg Sawdde Common in Llangadog, haven't you?" asks Rhys. "You must keep your hands on it or the landowners will pinch it. It only takes a word in the right ear in the government up in London, then they can put up walls and gates and throw the ordinary man out of his cottage."

The many growls and bangings of clenched fists on the bar tables speak of their agreement.

"Did you hear about the trouble in Llangadog first thing this morning, then ...?"

Chapter 18

Elin leaves her home as the first rays of the sun are peeping over the Black Mountain and kissing the stone walls of the pub.

"I'm pleased that Haden can come with us," says Elin. "At least she'll be company for me when I leave you two far behind."

"This morning isn't a fair test," Siôn replies. "We had so much food last night."

"To say nothing of the wonderful beer ..." says Harri. "And I noticed that you went to bed early. Even before Gwyndaf got home."

" Where are we going first?" Elin asks.

"Rhys has arranged that the farmers bring their its sheep together in one field – Cwm Gwenllan, this side of Capel Gwynfe," Harri says.

"We'll go up the road to Pantmeinog and over towards Pant-y-grafog, then," says Elin. "We can cross the river Sawdde below Godre'r-waun. You only need to follow Nant Gwenllan upstream then."

"You know the paths, fair play to you, *croten*," Siôn says.

"Off we go then!" Elin takes off her clogs and pushes her hands into them, as usual, as the two stockmen look on in amazement. But when they see her running, unhindered, ahead of them Siôn and Harri do the same. Haden is in her element, of course, her tongue lolling out and Elin could swear she's giggling as she trots along with them.

"How far is it from here to Cwm Gwenllan, then?" Siôn asks.

"About three miles."

He shuts up then, saving his breath for running. Even though drovers walk about twelve or fifteen miles a day when droving, and the stockmen do far more as they dart this way and that, controlling the animals, they're used to doing it at a fairly leisurely pace. There's no advantage to be gained by making the cattle and sheep walk too fast – they'd reach the market as skin and bone. It would be the same as taking empty baskets to sell. If they do need to put on a quick spurt, there's always time to catch their breath soon afterwards.

But there's no rest for them running with Elin that morning. These lads are tough and can go all day, every day for three weeks, and more sometimes, she thinks. But can they run over a long distance? Over the last few weeks, she's run this route several times with Beca messages for Lowri Pant-y-grafog. The road rises a fair bit in the first mile and then follows the contour for the second mile, more or less all the way to Lowri's home. She decides to put some pressure on the boys over the first mile.

At half a mile, she and Haden have left the stockmen far behind. This is a new experience for them. Then, when they reach the Pantmeinog junction, they have a choice – left or right.

"Which way did she say?" says Siôn, flopping to rest against the hedge.

"No idea! Call Haden."

The two men call and whistle for their dog and Haden starts barking from the spot where Elin has gone to hide behind Pantmeinog's stable. She lets the dog free and then emerges herself, a mischievous smile her face.

"Yes, alright, we can see that you can run!" says Siôn.

"Take it steady from here, Elin. We don't want to be back too soon or Rhys will send us to Llanddeusant to fetch another flock this afternoon."

"It's easier going from here on, *bois*. Follow the slope round and then a sharp turn above the river Sawdde."

As Elin reaches Pant-y-grafog, Lowri hurries out of the house on spotting her.

"Is there a message, Elin? Is something supposed to happen? Has something happened?"

"Not today, Lowri. Haven't heard anything about next week yet. We're droving today. We'll be back through with a flock of sheep this afternoon."

"Oh, I see. Are these dogs good workers for you, Elin?" Lowri asks, looking playfully at Haden and then at the two young men.

"This red bitch is pretty good," Elin says, patting Haden's head, "but there's work to be done training these two young pups!"

And that sets the tone for the rest of the day, with Elin enjoying pulling the boys' legs in front of the shepherds from around Capel Gwynfe.

"Oh, yes, we've suspected for years that there wasn't much go in Rhys Prydderch's lads, haven't we, *bois*?" says one of the farmers as he adds his sheep to the ever-growing flock. "You have to be quick to get the best price in the market and we've noticed that the prices have been low for a year or more!"

By mid-afternoon the three of them are back at Tafarn y Wawr with the sheep. Elin has to go and help in the kitchen. Before supper time news arrives from the village, carried by Dan Dowlais. By this time the pub is packed with more farmers and their farmhands, catching up with the drovers' tales.

"I was in the village this afternoon, hanging the new gate at the vicarage," Dan says. "I saw it all with my own eyes."

"What was that, Dan?"

"That Richard Chandler."

"What did he do, Dan?"

"He came out of his house, past me and through the gate. On then to the vicarage and in to see the vicar. The front door was opened before he'd gone up the steps to the house. Someone had summoned him there, I'd say – they were expecting him. He was in there for over an hour."

"Yes, what happened then, Dan?"

"*Jiawch*, this here tankard's pretty empty, *bois* ..."

"Elin, fetch the jug and pour Dan another, would you. Here you go, the money's just here on the table."

"Well," Dan continues, after wetting his whistle. "When he came out, he looked pretty crestfallen. You could tell by the way he walked. He went into his own house and before long Heddwenna, the cook, came out with a bag in her hand and she gave a right mouthful to someone who asked what was going on. Catrin the under-housemaid looked relieved when he was going. Then a servant came out of the vicarage stable with a horse and cart. They waited outside Chandler's house. He came out like a shot and barked some order to the servant. He went in then and had to carry two trunks out to the cart. Chandler climbed up into the back and sat on the crosswise seat and then the servant gave the horse a prod and off they went, wherever they were going."

"We've seen the back of him in this parish, *bois*," one of the farmers says.

"Well, at least he didn't get sent to the workhouse, unlike some," says another.

"Becca's done her work once again, I'd say," adds yet another.

The conversation goes on in the same vein, with the achievements of Rebecca and her Daughters listed, much to the delight and pride of the group gathered there.

When Gwyndaf returns, Elin shoots over to him and whispers, "Down the cellar. Now. I've got some news."

In the complete stillness of the cellar, Elin shares the latest about Richard Chandler.

"Where did you go to?" she asks her brother. "Have you got any news for me?"

"From Anna. And her mother. I've got something to tell you. Sit on that barrel, Elin. It's not a nice story."

"What d'you mean? Has something happened?"

"Yes. Before our time. Eighteen years ago …"

"Eighteen years ago! The list on the warning!" Elin says. "Is that what you're saying?"

"Yes. Eighteen years ago …"

"The second thing on the list: 'bound her arms behind her in the wood ...'?"

"Yes."

There was a long pause.

Eventually, Gwyndaf says quietly, "Mari Lee was that woman. She told me to tell you. She wants you to understand ..."

"Mari Lee? He caught her? He tied her up ...? Oh, Mari! Mari *fach*!"

Elin holds her head in her hands. After a while she straightens up.

"I'm not surprised she threw that rock through his window ... twice!"

"She should have done something much worse to him and no one would have blamed her if she had," Gwyndaf says.

"Oh, that's why she said what she said about the toll-house children: 'Teach them to run fast, especially the girls.' Those were her words, Gwyndaf."

"She taught Anna how to run too. And you."

"I thought it was an old gypsy custom. But there's more to it than that."

"Yes. She wanted you to understand why things happened like they did in Llangadog yesterday."

"I'll go up to see her, first chance I get."

* * *

The drovers' days are busy ones. After the race to Capel Gwynfe, the lads want Elin's company and her knowledge of the trackways to Llanddeusant. The meeting place there is Maes-pant, and once again Elin is very familiar with the route to Pant-y-gwin, about three-quarters of the way there, where she regularly passes on Beca's messages to Idris, the farmer's son.

"This one knows everyone in the county!" Siôn says in amazement, seeing her have a quick chat with the son in the farmyard.

When they're on their way back to Llangadog with the sheep, Elin looks across from the hills towards the Black Mountain before heading down into Cwm Llwyn-y-bedw.

"There's no sign of the Mountain," warned the other stockman. "There's a black cloud on top of it. There'll be rain before nightfall."

By the skin of their teeth, the three of them and Haden manage to drive the sheep quickly enough to get them into the pub's fields as the first drops fall.

"This rain is summer storm rain," says Rhys Prydderch. "There'll be floods after this. We won't be able to start out tomorrow morning, as we'd hoped. The streams and rivers will be too high."

Because the drovers aren't willing to pay the tolls to use the turnpike roads and bridges, they have to wait for favourable weather so that they can use fords to cross the streams on their journey. Walking sheep in wet weather is much more hazardous work than walking cattle. The heavy rain sets in for days. The hill farms seem to shrink and shelter lower in the land every day, for days.

"There's nothing worse than low cloud and fog when

you're trying to follow a mountain path," Rhys Prydderch says. "You can lose an entire flock in those conditions. Pooft! Gone in an instant."

"To say nothing of water *on* the land," Harri says. "Some paths turn into rivers, and ..." – he shoots a sly glance over at the old drover – "not everyone's mounted on a pony!"

It is Tuesday morning when the flock gets underway on its journey. Harri's in front and sixty sheep follow him, then sixty more follow Siôn. Rhys Prydderch, on his pony, is at the back making sure there are no stragglers and Haden is everywhere. It's quite a sight, but Elin in longing for the hurly-burly of their departure to disappear round the bend in the road so she can escape to Coed yr Arlwydd.

Although it's still early, she knows that Mari will be out in front of her gypsy tent in the clearing.

She runs all the way, sweating as she climbs the hill. When she sees Elin, Mari stands up to meet her and embrace her. She feels the heat from the runner warm her cold body. The tears on Elin's cheeks cleanse her.

* * *

Elin and Gwyndaf go over every day that week. Tom and Jorjo are still finding haymaking work on the hill farms, so there is no mention of the summer encampment ending.

"And the corn harvest will be starting soon," Gwyndaf says. He knew that many extra hands would be needed to tie up and carry the sheaves. But then again, he understood that travel was a gypsy's life. The different seasons meant different pathways for them. When the pub is at its busiest – when the drovers are preparing for their September and October journeys – the gypsies would be moving into Herefordshire to work in the apple and hop harvests.

And the summer isn't over yet. One morning in very early August, Tom arrives with news from a farm in Cwm Cennen, where he's been working in the haymaking.

"There was big trouble on Llandybïe Common Monday night," he says.

"Trouble?" Elin says.

"Beca," Tom says.

"Is there a toll-gate there, then?"

"Knocking walls down. The walls that are being built round the land that's being stolen by the estate."

"Knocking down a wall! That's a bit more work than smashing up a gate!" Gwyndaf says.

"Rebecca left a message saying that enclosing the common is taking away the rights of ordinary people in the area, rights that have been there for centuries," says Tom.

"The people have the rights, not London," Mari Lee insists.

"It's an awful thing when they steal your land from you," says Jorjo. "They steal the roads, steal the mountain, steal the common. We gypsies know full well what's happening. We're a people who have lost our land too."

"We have to make sure they can't steal Carreg Sawdde Common," Elin says.

"Nor Coed yr Arlwydd," Jorjo adds. "Llew the blacksmith told me that at one time the name was Coed yr Arglwydd –

the Lord's wood. He said that this common land was given by Rhys Ieuanc, the Lord of Castell Meurig – the old castle above the river Sawdde – so that the people of this area could benefit from it.

"We'll keep it safe, don't you worry," Elin says.

And no one was going to argue with her that night.

Chapter 19

"This one will be the big night," Llew tells Elin, in the smithy stable on the Wednesday. "We'll be out all night. We'll be purging the whole valley of gates."

"What are the three trees, then?" asks Elin.

"Friday the fourth of August. Rhyd-y-saint. Ten o'clock."

"Would it be a good idea to add another tree – 'All night'? That would give them notice to prepare."

"It would. You're right, Elin. And say that everyone who can come on a horse or a pony is to do so."

"And ten o'clock is early?"

"Got to be. It's going to be a bit of a trek, you see. We'll be starting with the Pont-ar-llechau Gate—"

"Going up the valley, are you? Are you sure I'm supposed to know all this?"

"It's important you know, Elin. In case ..."

"In case what?"

"In case things go amiss. You see, we'll be continuing up the valley and smashing the Black Mountain gates ..."

"Could you get caught and cornered by doing that?"

"Exactly. If the Dragoons come after us to the head of the valley, we'll be like mice in a trap. But Iori Plough Inn says the Dragoons' plans have already been made – the Llandeilo Dragoons will be going towards Pumsaint through Talley and the Llan'dyfri Dragoons will be heading to the same place via

Llanwrda. They've swallowed the story that there's going to be a rumpus in Pumsaint on Friday night. They think they'll trap them with a pincer movement – the swords closing in on Rebecca and her Daughters from two directions."

"How did you get them to swallow the lie, then?"

"We've been working on this for weeks. Since the start. They trust the person who's feeding them information—"

"Before you go any further, Llew," Elin says, interrupting, "I have to share something I've noticed too. It's difficult for me to say this, but with things more risky than usual Friday night, it's important that there isn't a traitor among the Daughters, isn't it?"

"Yes. You're quite right. But I wouldn't have thought that there's a traitor—"

"Forgive me, Llew." Elin glances towards the smithy door, behind which they can hear Dan working. "Little things I've seen with my own eyes. They throw suspicion on Dan ..."

"Dan?"

Quickly and anxiously, Elin tells him of all the suspicious interactions she's noticed between Dan and the authorities. She apologises profusely to the blacksmith for tainting his son like this, but she says she feels he ought to know. After she's finished, she sees the old smith bury his face in his hands and thinks he's about to cry ...

But he bursts out laughing, until his whole body is shaking.

"Dan! Dan!" calls the smith and Elin is mortified when Dan comes and opens the stable door.

"Dan – you know I told you to be careful that no one saw

you when you had your little meetings with the Dragoons and Bishop."

"Yeah."

"Well, there's one pair of eyes that clocked you fair and square! She doesn't miss a trick!"

"Did she now?" Dan winks at her. "You're eagle-eyed, aren't you, Elin?"

"It's Dan who's laid the false trail for the Dragoons," Llew explains. "But first, he had to be accepted as a dependable traitor ..."

"But he sent the Dragoons to Coed yr Arlwydd after the Glan Sawdde Gate got smashed. They could easily have caught Dicw."

"Dan had been up to warn Jorjo first. They were expecting the Dragoons. They were playing into the game too, you see ..."

"But Pumsaint ... the Dragoons could have caught Beca that time if I hadn't ..."

"Striking early and hiding was the intention all along," explains Llew. "The Dragoons believed Dan and thought they'd just had bad luck that night."

"So Dan's told them about going to Pumsaint again on Friday night?"

"Yes, and they'll be there earlier this time. The gates have been replaced. So, they've swallowed it hook, line and sinker. Iori's confirmed it."

"But what about Dan?" Elin asks. "Won't they know he's deceived them?"

"Dan's going to Merthyr tomorrow. The excuse is he's going to order more iron. He won't be back for three weeks, so he can say that Beca changed the plan while he was away."

Elin mulls the whole thing over. Then she nods her head and smiles.

"It's very clever! It's worked like a dream. So the Llangadog Beca is safe?"

"As safe as the Bank of the Black Ox!"

"And we're sure there's no one carrying stories?"

"No, because Dan is such a good 'traitor', they haven't sought out anyone else in the area, you see," says the blacksmith with a chuckle. "There are no traitors in Llangadog or the rest of the Sawdde valley. No one's carrying tales to the authorities, we can be sure of that. After smashing the Black Mountain gates, we'll be coming back smartish along the Sawdde valley road, hitting the Llangadog Gate again, and the one at Pont ar Dywi, and finish off by ridding Carreg Sawdde Common of its gate. Nine gates in one night!"

"There's another thing, Llew," says Elin.

"She has more to say! Beca must be pleased that this one's on her side!"

"The Powells, who keep the toll-gate at Pont Carreg Sawdde – they have small children. If the father doesn't have work, they'll be in the workhouse ..."

"Beca will be asking him – Simon Powell – to stop charging a toll on the bridge ever again," Dan says.

"I know she will. But Beca's against the workhouse too," Elin says. "She's against all injustice. And I've been thinking ..."

"Yes, out with it, Elin," Llew says.

"There's a vacancy at the church. Chandler's left. Bookkeeping, accounting, being fairer when the church goes to collect money from parishioners – a toll-keeper should be able to do all that."

"You're right," says the blacksmith. "Beca could leave a note on the door of the vicarage on Friday night—"

"Saying that his new gates will be in the river Tywi, and the trees in the garden felled before his son's party on Sunday if he doesn't listen!"

"Elin's thought it all out, Dan!"

"Go and tell that man with the black cravat to write the notice then!" she says.

"How on earth did you know that it's ..."

Elin laughs and heads for the door.

* * *

Outside the smithy she is surprised to see Mari Lee walking towards her across the meadow.

"I was told you'd be here," she says to Elin, once she's close enough. "Come with me."

She walks on across the common and then turns towards Rhyd-y-Saeson. Although Elin questions her, the gypsy doesn't say much.

When they reach the ford, Mari Lee looks carefully at the water in the river.

Before long she says, "The level's gone down now, after all that rain last week."

"It has. But I don't understand what that's got to do with me ..."

"You have to take notice of dreams," Mari Lee says,

turning to face her. "D'you remember me telling you?"

"Yes, but—"

"Last night, I had a dream about you. You were running through *pani*, through water. Now, I don't want to know, I don't want you to say anything. But there's a message in the dream. I brought you here so you could practise. The river's only half way up your shins today. You'll be alright. If you can hear the water singing as it flows over the stones in the ford, it's safe. It's a quiet river that's dangerous. That's when the water is deep. So, take off your clogs and run across the river."

Elin does as she is told and tries to run through the flow. Although it isn't deep, moving quickly is difficult. She turns to look back at Mari Lee, laughing as she raises her legs high, splashing water over her clothes.

"Don't lift your feet out of the water!" the gypsy shouts to her. "Push your way through rather than lifting your legs out. Keep your legs straight."

Elin acts on the advice. Although she doesn't feel like she's running, she realises that she's moving faster.

"Now, come back doing the same thing again!" shouts Mari Lee to her, once she's reached the opposite bank. She insists she does this three times.

"You must feel the stones on the riverbed with your feet. Can you do that?"

"Yes, if I concentrate," Elin says.

"Come here." The gypsy takes off a colourful cotton sash she is wearing and ties it across Elin's eyes.

"Now, I want you to follow the riverbank, in the shallow

water. It's not even up to your ankles. Run along the river first. It doesn't matter if you splash. Go faster! Right – turn, and come back as fast as you can. Keep feeling the stones with your feet. You must gain confidence if you're not going to fall."

Mari Lee pushes her without rest for half an hour, but eventually calls to her to stop and take the blindfold off.

"What was all that about?" says Elin, once she's got her breath back.

"I dreamed you were running at night."

"Running at night as well as through water?"

"Yes."

"That's very odd, Mari Lee."

"Dreams *are* odd. You go out tonight to practise running at night. And tomorrow night too."

* * *

By Friday afternoon, Elin has practised running in the dark two nights in succession. That afternoon, as she is preparing to go out round the valley to spread the word about Beca's summons that night, it starts raining.

Mari Lee's dream was right: the pathways will be wet, she says to herself. But she was mistaken about me running at night.

Even so, she is thankful for the training on wet rocks.

She keeps up her speed and doesn't fall over, either. She shares the message, but this time an odd feeling gnaws away at her. She can't help but think of Rachel, Mei and Dafy in the little toll-house by the bridge.

She helps Gwyndaf into her bonnet and one of her nightgowns, but there isn't the usual thrill of getting ready. She watches him leave the yard a little after half past nine. It's important he shouldn't be late that night ...

She feels the lump in her guts tighten. Then she makes a quick, determined decision. There'll be no turning back.

She puts on her shawl and goes out into the yard. The afternoon's showers have turned to drizzle by now. She starts running down the road to the village. She turns and follows a field path. She crosses the main Dyffryn Sawdde road and runs towards the bridge on the common. She knocks on the door of the toll-house.

When Simon Powell answers the door, his greeting is curt.

"There's no charge for pedestrians to go through the gate, *croten*. Don't be disturbing me for nothing—"

"Quick, bring me the children," Elin says. On her way down from the pub, she has been preparing in her head what she's going to say. "Nona, your wife, can come with them to. They'll be safe then."

"What are you on about? Are you mad?"

"There's no time to argue. Do what I say. NOW!"

On hearing raised voices at the door, his wife comes out to see what the fuss is about.

"You can have the drovers' room at Tafarn y Wawr for tonight," she explains. "But there's no time to lose. Fetch the children at once."

Nona Powell grasps what's afoot and turns without question to go and rouse the children.

"How do you know? What's going on ...?"

"It's nothing personal against you, don't worry about it,"
Elin says. "Just show a bit of respect. Men in other toll-houses
have behaved like gentlemen. And keep this in mind: Beca
looks after her own. There'll be a new post for you after this,
of that I'm sure."

"Beca! But ...? Another post ...?"

"Behave respectfully," Elin reiterates. "If you do, you and
your family won't end up in the workhouse. Mark my words!"

The children and their mother appear. Rachel recognises
her and smiles.

"Who'd like to run in the night?" Elin asks them in an
excited tone.

"Me! Me! Me!"

"Come on then! Let's cross the bridge first ..."

As she crosses back over the bridge, Elin looks towards
the village. Heddwenna, the cook, is standing beside the
stone wall of Glan Sawdde, staring at them, her hands like
two enormous wooden spoons by her sides.

Chapter 20

"That's exactly what Gwladys would have done," Tegwen Rees says to Elin when she comes downstairs, once mother and children are settled in the drovers' bedroom. Tegwen and Brython Rees are sitting at the big table in their homely kitchen. They are holding hands.

"What's the matter with you two?" asks Elin, gesturing with a nod of her head at their entwined fingers on the table. "And what's this about Gwladys?"

"Sit down, Elin," her father says. "The time has come. Your mother and I have something to share with you."

She sits down in tense silence.

"My sister, Gwladys ..." Brython says. "She was your mother ..."

"What ...? But you are my ..." She looks at Tegwen and sees her eyes filling with tears.

"Fifteen years ago, Gwladys wasn't married. She was a very pretty young woman," says Brython. "Blonde hair, blue eyes, an athletic body, tall too – just like you. But something horrific happened to her. She was a maid at the vicarage ..."

Elin's hand flies to her mouth and her face turns deathly white.

"Oh no!" Her breath comes fast and shallow. She puts her elbows on the table and holds her head in her hands. Then she raises her head and looks first into mother's eyes, then her father's. "You don't mean 'ruined one of the vicarage maidservants by defilement', do you ...?"

"Yes, *fach*," Tegwen says, reaching across the table to grasp both of Elin's hands in her own. "It was him who made Gwladys pregnant. And she died ..."

Weeping, Tegwen brings her hands back to cover her own face. She cannot manage another word.

After a long silence, Elin hears her father's voice. It is shaky and filled with emotion.

"Gwladys died giving birth to you, Elin. She'd come back here to us as soon as she knew she was expecting a baby. We looked after her. You were born in the drovers' bedroom."

"And you two brought me up ...? But Gwyndaf ...? Was she expecting twins ...?

"No," says Tegwen. "I was expecting at the same time, you see. I think the shock of your birth and losing Gwladys moved things along. Gwyndaf was born the next day. We told everyone that Gwladys' baby had died at the same time as its mother ..."

"... and that Tegwen had given birth to twins," adds Brython.

"And we were raised as brother and sister?" asks Elin.

"You two are exactly like twins, at least as far as understanding each other," Tegwen says.

There is another heavy silence in the kitchen as Elin tries to take in the news. She lifts her head and looks them both in the eye, one after the other.

"And you two are wholly my mother and father," she says. "Nothing can change that."

More tears fall from Tegwen's eyes, and Brython is filling up too.

"And no one else knows about this?" asks Elin.

"The whole neighbourhood knew what Chandler had done to Gwladys, and everyone knew she was pregnant," says Brython.

"Only the midwife knows the lot. The one who came here to try and help Gwladys and then to help me," says Tegwen.

"Is she still alive?"

"Mari Lee," Brython says.

Elin lets out a deep sigh. Waves of different emotions roll over each other. She immediately understands why she feels a deep bond between her and the gypsy.

But the conversation comes to a sudden halt.

The door of the pub bursts open. Ianto Tal-y-garn comes in.

"Elin. You must go. Message for Beca. Quick ... O, *bois bach* ..."

Ianto struggles for breath. Elin places a chair for him to sit down on. His lungs are burning after running there as fast as he could. Elin tries to work out where Rebecca and her Daughters are by now. Meet at Rhyd-y-saint. Going straight for Pont-ar-llechau. Those on foot doing the work there. Half of those on horseback to go through Capel Gwynfe towards the Cwm Llwyd Gate, the other half towards the Pont Clydach Gate – both of those factions some three miles further on from Pont-ar-llechau, both at the foot of the Black Mountain. The Daughters would be in three groups by now ...

"Iori sent a message." Ianto goes into more detail once he's got his breath back. "The Llandeilo Dragoons changed their plans late in the day. Maybe the original plan was a set-up. The Llan'dyfri Dragoons are still going to Pumsaint, but the Llandeilo ones are going to go over the bridge to Llangadog and on towards the mountain gates."

A trap! thinks Elin. The three groups will be cornered at the head of the valley.

"What time are they leave Llandeilo?" asks Elin.

"Iori's message left Llandeilo at nine. The Dragoons are due to leave at half past ten."

"Why have the Dragoons changed their plans?" Elin asks him slowly and apprehensively.

"They got a message, according to Iori," Ianto replies. "He suspects it was a message from Llangadog ..."

Heddwenna the cook! thinks Elin. But then comes a rush of uncertainties pounding in her head. What if her action – taking the Pont Carreg Sawdde toll-house children to safety – has betrayed Beca's plans to Heddwenna? And she, of all people, has led all the Daughters into a trap?

Elin rushes to the door. Her mother is there before her.

"Take care, Elin. Take the greatest possible care!"

"I will ..." She turns to look into her mother's eyes. "I will, Mam, but I don't have much time."

She goes out into the yard. Then through the fields towards Pont Goch, thinking all the while. Gwyndaf has taken the pony that night. The grass is damp. She's familiar with the path but she can't see her feet. But she must hurry. She pushes herself on, even though she often slips and loses her footing.

Gradually, her eyes become accustomed to the dark.

There's a half-moon, but the sky's cloudy.

As she approaches Pont Goch Cottage, she sees a dark shadow moving in front of the house. By now the estate has let it to new tenants. Strangers. From a different area. She doesn't know them. It's clear the estate thinks them suitable. She tries to make as little noise as possible as she runs.

Suddenly, she sees a shadow coming towards her. It's a dog! The cottage dog. A strange dog. The new tenants' dog. She tries to think. Tries to remember. Her father had told her something once. Look straight into a dog's eyes! – yes, that was it. Don't show you're afraid! And try and hit it on its nose. The shadow gets closer, and it's speeding up. It's a big, muscular dog. As it jumps up, she raises her hand and smacks it hard on the nose with the clog she is wearing on her right hand. Her timing is perfect. The dog drops, howling. She leans over and gives it another whack on the nose with her left clog. Anger surges through her, giving her blows extra force. She looks at the dog, cowering with its belly to the ground and feels no mercy. Chandler's character coming out in me, she thinks – but she pushes the thought away as soon as it occurs to her.

The cottage door opens. There's someone holding a candle and shouting into the dark. Elin turns and carries on running. She has already decided to turn to the left and go up the valley. She might be making a big mistake. If the first group of Daughters, the ones on foot, have already passed and are making their way to the village, they'll come face to face with the Dragoons. But she has to take the chance. Would the dog have been running free if the Daughters had already passed? She runs at a gallop now. Every second counts. The road is smooth – a turnpike road. Although there are dark trees on the valley slopes either side of the road, she can see the road surface fairly clearly. As she passes Melin-y-cwm, she can hear voices. She hears a horn. The Daughters! They are coming towards her. They are safe for now.

As she reaches the turn at Pont Fawr, she comes face to face with the first band. There are about a hundred of them, in high spirits.

"Go back! Go back!" Elin shouts.

The procession stops.

"What's up? What's the matter?"

"Oh, it's Elin!"

"Are you alright, Elin?"

"The Dragoons are coming up this road ... before long ... You have to turn back ... Go back towards Rhyd-y-saint ... then you can go along the road for Cefn-y-coed and Coed yr Arlwydd."

"But how is it that the Dragoons—?"

"There's no time to explain now!" screams Elin. "Go back! At once!"

"You heard the girl," says the voice at the front of the crowd. "Quick! Turn back. Now. Run. And quietly. Everyone quiet."

"How many of you are here?" Elin asks. "Where are the ones on horseback?"

"Oh, they've been gone for an hour or more. They're not far behind us, I wouldn't think. The two mounted groups are supposed to meet at Pont-ar-llechau."

"Head for Coed ar Arlwydd and hide there," Elin says.

Elin hears the sound of feet starting to run. The whole valley echoes to the sound of clogs pounding along the road.

"Keep quiet!" she yells. "You'll be safe there. I'll go on to meet the horses."

"No, Elin! One of us can run with the message."

"Huh! Run in a petticoat!" says Elin dismissively. "I know the road, I'm used to running it. I'll be quicker ..."

Without wasting any more time arguing, Elin darts past the men, over the bridge, past Rhyd-y-saint and runs along the road running below Allt-y-fedw.

When she is half way along this flat stretch, she hears the sound of horns in front of her. Thank goodness – Rebecca! She stands in the middle of the road, waiting for the horses to arrive.

"Woah! Woah!" calls the rider at the front. "Stop! There's someone ... There's a girl ...!"

The pack comes to a halt. Rebecca herself comes forward to see what is the matter.

"Elin! What are you doing here?"

"Llew ... Is everyone here – the groups from both gates?"

Elin gives him her message. She lets out a whoop of delight on hearing that the gangs from both gates are back together in one group.

"We'll have to go back to Pont-ar-llechau!" Llew shouts. "We'll go another way. Maybe through Gwynfe ...?"

"No!" shouts Elin. "Some of the Dragoons are bound to come through Gwynfe. They're heading for the mountain gates. And once they see that the Pont-ar-llechau's been smashed, their swords will be out ..."

"What do you suggest, then?"

"Pont-ar-llechau ... turn left, over the river, onto the Ffinnant road ... take the turning for Caeau Bychain's farmyard ... then follow the track through the fields and hide out in Coed Caeau Bychain. You'll be able to see the road from those woods but they won't be able to see you. Is Gwyndaf with you?"

"Yes, he's safe at the back with the lads that came back from Cwm Llwyd." says Llew. "Right! Turn round, *bois*!" he shouts. "You jump up here with me on my pony, Elin," he says to her.

"No, two of us will slow the pony up. He's run enough already. I'll cross the river here. There's a path through Allt Caeau Bychain woods back to Rhyd-y-saint. I'll go and tell the other lot to stay put in Coed yr Arlwydd until they get word from you."

Elin watches the horses and ponies galloping away up the valley. She has done her work. She stands in the middle of the road, savouring the moment. Then she hears a sound like distant thunder behind her. Hoofs! The Dragoons – they are on their way! Beca won't have enough time to make the turn at the bridge and disappear up the Ffinnant road.

She stands her ground in the middle of the road. She can see the first cavalrymen at the far end of the flat stretch. Stand your ground, she says to herself. She hears the voice of the officer barking a command in the distance – he's seen her! She hears the sound of metal scraping against metal – they are unsheathing those long swords!

Elin turns and runs to the right and scrambles up on top of the wall. She jumps down the other side. The river is a few feet away. She wades into the water. This is no ford; this is a river full of pools and rugged rocks. She pushes herself forward. She is up to her waist in the water and the water is cold, straight off the mountain, even though it is August. She pushes her legs through it. She feels the rough surface of the stones on the riverbed with her feet.

Then, they feel nothing. She has stepped into a deep pool. She pushes her body forward. She feels the river carrying her. She feels the riverbed once more. She straightens her body. She can hear the Dragoons slowing down. They have reached the spot where she'd jumped over the wall. She must reach the bank. She can see a big rock on the bank. She must get shelter between herself and the road ...

She hears the voice barking commands. She hears clicking ... they are cocking their guns. Then she feels the level of water receding down her legs. She's crossed the river! She surges ahead and feels dry land under her feet. She jumps from stone to stone and flings herself behind a large rock under the canopy of trees on the bank.

"Fire!"

Twenty guns spurt sparks and smoke and Elin hears the lead shots whistling over the river and hitting tree trunks and stones along the bank. She crouches in the shelter of the large rock. Silence. Only the sound of the river.

The captain shouts, "Something, something ... only a girl ...", but Elin doesn't understand the rest.

In any event, she knows she's delayed the Dragoons long

enough for the Daughters of Rebecca to escape. They will have heard the shooting and will have had enough time to grab the toll-keeper and take him with them to hide on the Ffinnant road.

She stays behind the rock, her clothes soaking wet, for several long minutes. She hears the Dragoons start moving again, then galloping along the road, then the sound of their bugles and the hoofs slowing down, then stopping.

They're at Pont-ar-llechau, she thinks. She hopes – she prays – that they go on and don't split up to search each road leading from that crossroads. Hopefully, their intention to trap Beca at the head of the valley will win out.

Maybe they'll make inquiries in the pubs and in the smithy and at the cooper's house in the hamlet of Pont-ar-llechau. There's a Rebecca supporter in every house so they're sure to send the Dragoons onwards.

After what feels like and age, she hears galloping hoofs once more. She listens to the sound slowly receding up the valley.

* * *

Elin has reached Coed yr Arlwydd. She has walked along the bottom of the wooded slope to Rhyd-y-saint with no trouble, and it was then a small matter to cross back across the river and follow the road to the common. There, the Daughters are hiding in the woods.

Everyone wants to know what the sound of gunfire was about, and there is relief all round when the Daughters hear that no one has been hit. The group waits patiently. Eventually, everyone hears the Dragoons pass for the second time.

"They're sure to take a squint at Carreg Sawdde Common," says one of the Daughters beside her. "When they see that every gate in Llangadog is safe, they'll think it's all over."

An hour has passed, thinks Elin. She hears a noise. Hoofs! She quickly realises that these are the hoofs of Rebecca and her Daughters. She moves forward to meet them.

Llew is at the front.

"Is Elin with you? We heard the rifles ... Is she alright? Does anyone know anything?"

Elin hears the concern in the blacksmith's voice. She's sure they were all worried when they'd heard the sound of shots ... Then she sees her brother on their pony.

"Gwyndaf!" She makes her way into the road, threading her way between Beca's horses.

"Elin!" She hears the relief in the lad's voice. Gwyndaf jumps down from the pony and hugs his twin.

Chapter 21

"No," Llew says decisively. "You're to take your sister home. She's soaked through. She's saved Beca tonight."

The Daughters had had a quick discussion and everyone had agreed that now was the safest time to clear away all the Llangadog gates. It was obvious the Dragoons had been disappointed and they would be on their way back to Llandeilo. They only had to ask at one or two houses on the common and in the village to confirm it.

"We shall soon possess the gates of those who hate us!" Llew says. "They've got my name down in the book at the Rhyd-y-Saeson Gate. I can't wait to get my hands on it! I'll be using it to light the fire in the smithy tomorrow morning!"

But Gwyndaf is forbidden to go on with the others.

"Your job is to look after this *croten*," Llew says to him emphatically. "Elin's run faster than the swords and saved us from being caught like sitting ducks."

After telling Llew the whole story, Elin says she thinks it is she who is to blame for the Dragoons changing their plans.

"No," Llew answers firmly. "It's Heddwenna who has betrayed us. She'll be hearing from us. It's you, Elin, who has saved us. Now, off you go, you two – down through the wood to Pont Goch. Look after her, Gwyndaf. Good night."

The twins see the crowd move off towards Carreg Sawdde Common. By now the gang's spirits have been reinvigorated with infectious jollity. But no one is shouting and there is no firing of guns or sounding the horns – just in case.

Elin climbs up onto the mare and sits in front of Gwyndaf. How nice to feel his arms round her as he holds the reins, she thinks. As they pass the path leading to the clearing, they see a shadow beside a tree. They see someone standing there ... a woman ...

"Mari Lee!" calls Elin. "You were right! Running in the dark ... running through a river ... Your dream came true."

"I had another dream as I was falling asleep tonight, Elin," says Mari Lee. "I saw your mother and father crying ..."

"That was true too, Mari Lee," says Elin. "Gwyndaf, let me down for a minute ..."

Elin frees herself from her brother's arms. She slides off one side of the mare, runs to Mari Lee and hugs her. When Gwyndaf joins them, Elin puts her arm round his neck and pulls him in so that the three become one.

"Gwyndaf, did you know that Mari Lee delivered you and me into this world?"

* * *

The next morning, Elin goes down to Pont Carreg Sawdde with Nona Powell and the children. She knows that any sign of destruction is sure to affect the children. She tries to prepare them as they walk along the path through the fields.

"Oh, look at the sheep in this field!" Elin says as they reach the Cae-rhyn road. "And look at this wooden gate. The gate keeps the sheep safely in the field, doesn't it? Can you see that, Rachel?"

The little band moves on into the next field. There are cows in this one.

"And the gate keeps the cows safe here."

As they make their way down the path, Elin manages to turn the conversation towards the view in front of them.

"But people aren't the same as animals, are they, Mei?" She shakes her head. "How is a person different to an animal, Dafy?"

"We don't eat grass!"

"Very good, Dafy! What about you, Mei. What's the difference between people and animals?"

"We've got two legs and they've got four legs!"

"Very good, Mei. Rachel?"

"We're not kept in fields."

"Another good answer! We're free, we can come and go as we wish. And gates that treat us like animals shouldn't exist."

By now, they have reached the Sawdde valley main road. They can all see the Glan Sawdde toll-house in front of them. The gate has been smashed to bits, the roof of the toll-house pulled down again and parts of the walls have been destroyed. Elin sees a shiver go through Nona's body and she hears her inhale sharply. But we must prepare the children, thinks Elin.

"And look at the Glan Sawdde Gate," she says to them. "People are tired of being treated like animals, you see. The gate's been knocked down since last night and the people around here are free!"

Even so, she isn't at all comfortable as they turn onto the common to face Pont Carreg Sawdde and the toll-house that was, after all, the children's home. As they get nearer she sees with relief that no one has touched the roof of this house. The walls are standing. The gate, of course, is in splinters. Outside, Simon Powell is clearing up some of the mess. He seems to be completely unharmed.

"Here you are, back home!" he shouts merrily when he sees his children approaching. When he gets the chance, he whispers his thanks to Elin.

"I couldn't not," she replies. "Small children shouldn't have to face such a scene."

"I took your advice too, Elin. Thanks for that as well."

"And Rebecca was pleased with your courtesy?"

"Yes! I was allowed to retreat back indoors without anyone laying a finger on me."

"It's important that everyone remembers that, at the end of the day, they have to face their neighbours."

"Oh, and I had an unexpected message this morning," adds Simon Powell. "The vicar's servant came over. The vicar wants to see me this afternoon at two."

* * *

August was an eventful month. The Pontbren Araeth Gate was re-erected and pulled down again in no time. The ricks of corn at Newton House in Dinefwr Park were set on fire. There were more and more patrols of the Tywi valley by the Dragoons, and they kept a sharp eye on Llangadog and the Sawdde valley too. The main unrest moved to other areas. Rebecca and her Daughters still controlled the roads and surrounding countryside.

Elin continued to run with Rebecca's messages. But some other runners noticed that things were quieter, less lively than that busy night in the Sawdde valley. The Dragoons are taking a more sensible approach, they think. But violations of an older, different sort often fills Elin's thoughts these days.

On Wednesday the thirteenth of September, when things have been quiet in the neighbourhood for a while, Llangadog has another busy night. The gate on Carreg Sawdde Common is destroyed, as is the Pont-ar-llechau one, and another at Waun-Ystrad-Feurig. As soon as they are replaced with new gates, those are also destroyed.

Two days later, there is a lot of activity on Coed yr Arlwydd Common. Elin and Gwyndaf go up to the camp to help the family. This is the day they move off. The summer camp is being struck, the cart is being loaded and the family is moving east to the harvests of Herefordshire.

"Here we are, another summer gone," says Jorjo, having tossed the last basket onto the top of the load. "But the hazel rods have grown well this season. Did you see them? There's a good crop here. The leaves are starting to turn yellow now – but we'll be back next summer to cut them and make baskets for another Llandeilo fair!"

"Every journey is a circle," says Mari Lee.

Gwyndaf and Anna sit quietly, side by side, on a tree stump. Elin takes Dicw the pony over to the cart and hands his bridle to Jorjo.

"We'll miss Dicw in this valley, Jorjo!" she says. "He's a bit of a hero: hundreds of us think the world of this white pony and the woman who rides him!"

"Yes, well I think I got quite a bargain in the end from that Cardi at Llanybydder horse fair!"

"The will of the people who unite together is a good horse," says Mari Lee.

"And thanks for the running lessons, Mari Lee. I'm a different girl to how I was three months back."

"But you're the same Elin as you were when you were born," says Mari Lee, standing up and walking towards her to link arms with her.

Both women hear a noise on the path.

Elin is surprised to see Brython and Tegwen walking towards them. Brython is carrying one of the largest of the gypsy baskets over his arm.

"We couldn't thank you for the gift of this basket without filling it with things for the journey," Brython says.

Tegwen hands the contents to Mari Lee to stow in the cart.

"Wheaten bread, meat from one of the steers and *cawl* made with bone marrow," she says.

"Wheat as yellow as Elin's hair and a Welsh Black steer as dark as Gwyndaf's," says Mari Lee. "And they're all part of the wealth of Tafarn y Wawr."

* * *

Within a month, there is a large community meeting in the field below Coed yr Arlwydd. This is one of a series of mass gatherings to list complaints and petition for reform. Twelve hundred people fill the field, which is surrounded by woods.

At the start of the meeting, a warning is delivered to the crowd by the chairman: "Meetings to record the people's complaints have been condemned by the authorities as unlawful. They do not want to hear, they do not want to listen. They have guns and swords in this county and in several other counties of Wales to prevent us from voicing our views. Now, there are three ways into this field – two through the trees behind us, and one across the footbridge over the river Sawdde from the main road. If they – the Dragoons – come and if we need to escape their swords, don't go towards the river. The bridge is too narrow. Go into the woods. There are clearings in the woods, there is shelter under the branches. The common is a tiny piece of a free Wales which has been preserved for us here in the Sawdde valley for centuries. Before long, and that day can't come too soon, the roads in the valley, the country, and the whole of Wales will be free as well."

Turning to look about her during the applause, Elin sees that Dylan Lloyd and Thomas Foster are there. The Carmarthen journalist is speaking into the ear of the London man and he is scribbling furiously in his notebook. She turns a little further and sees Simon and Nona Powell and the children applauding. By now he is the parish official, living in Chandler's old house – and people are starting to say they are being treated justly by the local church at long last.

She looks over her other shoulder. Over in the middle of a group of strong men – the sort that could handle an axe or a sledgehammer, Elin thinks – are Llew Lewis and Dan Dowlais. Llew winks at her.

With Llew stands Jac from the Plough, Leisa, his wife, and Ann, his daughter, and a young lad. That must be Iori, Elin presumes – the lad working in the stables, the lad who overheard confidential information. Jac catches her eye and raises his hand towards his mouth, miming taking a drink from a tankard and then he points uphill, towards Tafarn y Wawr. Elin nods happily – it will be good to be serving him in her own pub later.

Three rows behind her, she sees Ianto Tal-y-garn and Siân Carregfoelgam standing together. Things seem to be going well there! Elin thinks. On seeing her, Ianto turns up his coat collar to hide his face and nods his head and gives her a stupid smile.

And there, at the back, leaning against the trunk of an oak tree, she sees the man in the black cravat. He catches her eye. He slightly lowers his head and raises his hand, giving her a quiet smile. The next time she looks in that direction, there is no one leaning against the oak tree.

Author's note

- ## The Daughters of Rebecca

The Rebecca Riots 1839–43 encompassed more than attacks on toll-gates across toll-roads, although over 240 gates in West Wales were destroyed during those years by hundreds of rioters dressed in women's clothes. Amongst the many causes of serious poverty amongst the ordinary people at this time was the tolls they were obliged to pay to travel the roads. As well as this, the price of food had risen; there was a succession of wet summers, leading to poor harvests; rents were high; and the churches demanded high payments of tithes. All the while, wages were low.

- ## The workhouse

Throughout the nations of Britain, there was a strong belief that there were two classes of people – the rich and powerful, who owned land, large estates, and industries, and the ordinary folk, who were poor and struggled to make a living and raise their families. Poverty was considered to be an offence. A new law was passed that forced poor people who failed to pay their rent and their debts to move out of their houses and into the workhouse, or poorhouse.

The workhouse was, effectively, a labour camp for the poor. Being put in the workhouse, a husband and wife could be separated – one sent to the women's section and the other to the men's. Children would be placed in a separate section.

Families might be separated for ever, without a hope of earning enough money to be released and reunited. The estate steward would have rented their old home to another family. Work was hard and repetitive in the workhouse: breaking rocks down to the size of gravel with which to make roads; walking a treadmill to power machinery; endless washing and mending; and chopping firewood. The food provided was worse than food in prison.

- **Other punishments**

Punishments for breaking the law were harsh and the prisons were filthy holes where prisoners starved. Often, for minor offences, men and women could be 'transported' – sent to British overseas colonies to work as forced labour on farms and in mineral mines on British territories, originally in America and, later, in Australia, South Africa, Canada and islands in the West Indies. Despite the courts stipulating a term of labour, few returned to Wales. For more serious offences, the hangman's rope was still in frequent use.

- **The Daughters of Rebecca against the workhouse**

On Monday 19 June 1843, large crowds gathered on the outskirts of Carmarthen to march behind a banner proclaiming 'CYFIAWNDER A CHARWYR CYFIAWNDER YDYM NI OLL' (justice, and lovers of justice are we all). Other banners read 'RHYDDID A GWELL LLUNIAETH' (freedom and better food) and 'TOLL RYDD A RHYDDID' (toll-free and freedom). A crowd of 10,000 attacked Carmarthen Workhouse, breaking windows and throwing furniture into the yard. The building would have been set on fire but was saved by the 4th Light Dragoons, led by Major William Parlby, who beat back the rioters with their long swords. One of the town's magistrates waved his hat in the air, urging the soldiers on: 'Slash away! Slash away!'

- **Soldiers against the common people**

When the ordinary people were provoked into rioting, the army would be called in to 'restore order'. In Britain, between 1739 and 1839, over 500 protesters were killed by the British army during various disturbances. In Wales, the worst of these were in Merthyr Tydfil in 1831 and in Newport in 1839. According to the court authorities, parliament and the army in Britain, the 'enemy' was often the common people.

- **The theft of common land**

A further cause of unrest in several parts of Wales was the 'enclosure' of common land. A 'common' is a piece of land where rights are held 'in common' by the ordinary people: woodland, for example, where the people of the parish had the right to collect firewood (a right called estovers) and turn out their pigs in the autumn to eat acorns and beech mast (pannage); it also includes mountain land where cattle could be grazed in the summer (pasture). Some commons were close to villages – like Carreg Sawdde Common near Llangadog. Animals would graze on the common and social activities could be held there. The gypsies were free to make camp on the common. A young couple, newly married, were able to build a '*tŷ unnos*' on common land – if they and their friends could build a house during one night and smoke could be seen rising from the chimney by dawn.

From about 1760, the practice of 'enclosing' common land – in other words, stealing it from the ordinary people – accelerated, effected by paying money to create an Act of Parliament in London. It was only landowners in their big houses who had the money to do this. Between 1795 and 1895, over a million acres of common land were taken from the ordinary people of Wales. Some lost their homes. Without the use of common land, some smallholdings were too small to support a family. Those who lost land were not compensated. The people of Wales lost their hold on fully a third of the country's land.

• The gypsies in Wales

People referred to as 'gypsies' have been familiar here in Wales since the Middle Ages. By around 1350, a network of fairs was held in the main towns in Wales and these would attract craftspeople, performers and nomadic families. Amongst them were dark-skinned people who often had a great love of music and were skilful in handling horses. They loved to dress in colourful clothes, with sparkling rings through their ears and on their fingers. They came to be known as 'gypsies', which is a corruption of 'Egyptians' – a misunderstanding about their place of origin. Their roots go back much further: their language can be traced back to India. They call themselves 'Roma', which means 'people'. They are close to nature, and know the secrets of the woods and of herbs. At first they lived in tents, and then in caravans, and they have suffered great prejudice and persecution because of being seen as different.

In Wales, many gypsy families learned to speak Welsh, and combined it with their own Romani language, creating a new Romani-Welsh language. When they spoke Welsh, they liked to create their own names for times, places and people. They wouldn't say 'mis Mai' (month of May), but 'mis y ddraenen wen' (month of the hawthorn); not 'Llangollen', but 'tref y cnau' (the town of nuts), because – although the town is really named after Saint Collen – the Welsh word for hazel nuts is 'cnau collen'; not Swansea, but 'dinas yr aderyn gwyn' (the city of the white bird), and policemen were called 'traed mawr' (big feet). So the sentence 'Daeth y traed mawr ar ein holau ni yn nhref y cnau ym mis y ddraenen wen, ac fe symudon ni i lawr i ddinas yr aderyn gwyn' (The big feet were after us in the town of nuts in the month of hawthorn, and we moved down to the city of the white bird) would mean nothing to Welsh people – but having a 'secret' language was a way for gypsies to protect themselves.

- **Fictitious characters**

Most of the characters in this novel are fictitious, but there is reference to Twn Carnabwth from Mynachlog-ddu, at the foot of the Preseli Mountains. Twm was the original 'Rebecca' that attacked the turnpike gates of West Wales in 1839. The 'man in the black cravat' is reminiscent of Hugh Williams, a solicitor who lived in Saint Clears and was a strong supporter of campaigns to secure justice for the common people. Some believe that he secretly planned some aspects of the Rebecca Riots. Another factual event included in this novel is that *The Times* sent Thomas Foster to West Wales to report on the unrest, and that his dispatches presented many of the people's complaints against the Establishment.

Most of the place names refer to real names, which can be located on a map, but the part they play in the story is made up. However, if particular dates are mentioned in the novel, the events on those days are part of the actual history of the Daughters of Rebecca in the Tywi valley.

Writing this story has also been a way for me to learn more about my predecessors, and to meet them – Jac Griffiths, the innkeeper and brewer at the Plough Inn is my great- great-great- grandfather; Leisa, his wife, is my great- great- great-grandmother; Ann, their daughter, is my great- great-grandmother and her fiancé, William Williams, Ffos-yr-efel, Pontarddulais, is my great- great- grandfather. The family history of being a '*teulu'r Beca*' (a Rebecca family) came down to me from my mother, and thanks to the Carmarthenshire Archive Service, I obtained much of their history. But I never met them, of course! I've fleshed the characters out on these factual bare bones.

- **Things that improved after the Rebecca Riots**

Many changes were soon seen in rural Wales after the Rebecca Riots. Travel was easier; by 1852, the railway had reached

Carmarthen and the toll-road system had been reformed. A few days after his arrival in Carmarthen, Colonel Love wrote a report to the government in London acknowledging that the West Wales people had reasonable complaints. There were too many toll-gates and the tolls were too high, he admitted. Within a fortnight, the Home Secretary had dispatched two researchers to Wales to look at the root of the problem. In October 1843, less than three months later, a Royal Commission was set up to thoroughly investigate the issue and collect testimony from witnesses in every town in south Wales and mid-Wales. The outcome of this was the passing of the South Wales Turnpike Trusts Act in August 1844, which resulted in much better and fairer system. All this happened because of the united stance and uncompromising action by Rebecca and her followers. In the same year, the Poor Law Amendment Act was passed; its main effect was to revise the treatment of unmarried mothers, reducing the numbers who ended up in the workhouse.

• The truth in the newspapers

Possibly one of the unsung heroes of this battle was Thomas Campbell Foster, correspondent for *The Times*. For the best part of a year he reported to this, the most influential London newspaper, based on the information he collected. He portrayed the wretched state of rural families and their oppression by landowners, magistrates and the ruling class. This was an innovative form of journalism, investigative in style and relentless, like a dog with a bone; it was brave to accept the evidence of ordinary people rather than that of the Establishment.

The spirit of Rebecca

It is likely that there were several local Rebeccas, and communication between the cells in different areas. Although a few influential people supported the riots in practical ways, the true heroes of the Daughters of Rebecca protests were the rural folk of West Wales – people – and yes, children – who dared to believe that they should live in a better country and who risked everything to forge a path to a fairer and more equal society.

In Wales, we still talk about the spirit of Rebecca. This is the spirit in people who are ready to stand up to unjust laws and tyrannical authority.

Running

Dylan Huws and Llion Iwan opened my eyes to the nature of ultra runners. This is a popular sport in Wales today, and Llion directed me to a very interesting book on the subject, *Born to Run* by Christopher McDougall (Profile Books, 2009), which reveals that such running is second nature to people. It would have been part of the way we hunted long ago, and women and older men are better and stronger, and have better stamina, than young men over distances of 50 to 100 miles. Another interesting fact is that a person's stride is more than a horse's when running.

Short bibliography

Molloy, Pat; *And they blessed Rebecca*, Gomer, Llandysul, 1983

Thomas, David; *Cau'r Tiroedd Comin*, Gwasg y Brython, Liverpool, 1952

Evans, Henry Tobit, Evans, Gwladys Tobit, Rice Trevor, George and Thomas, George; *Rebecca Riots!*, CreateSpace Independent Publishing Platform, 2010

The Carmarthen Journal, Carmarthenshire County Council Archives

Godwin, Fay & Toulson, Shirley; *The Drovers' Roads of Wales*, Wildwood House, London, 1977

Jarman, Eldra & A.O.H.; *Y Sipsiwn Cymreig*, Gwasg University of Wales Press, Cardiff, 1979

Jarman, Eldra & A.O.H.; *The Welsh Gypsies – Children of Abram Wood*, University of Wales Press, Cardiff, 1979

Le Bas, Damian; *The Stopping Places – a Journey through Gypsy Britain*, Vintage, London, 2018

Keet-Black, Janet; *Gypsies of Britain*, Shire Library, Oxford, 2018

Goodall, Peter J. R.; *The Black Flag over Carmarthen*, Gwasg Carreg Gwalch, Llanrwst, 2005

McDougall, Christopher; *Born to Run*, Profile Books, London, 2009

Novels steeped in history

Exciting and subtle stories based on key historical events

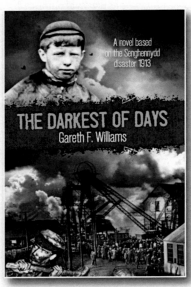

THE DARKEST OF DAYS
Gareth F. Williams

A novel based on the Senghennydd disaster 1913

£5.99

Shortly before 8.30 on the morning of 14 October 1913, 439 men and boys perished in a horrific explosion at Senghennydd coal mine.

John Williams was only eight years old when he and his family came from one of the slate mining villages of the north to live in Senghennydd, in the South Wales valleys. He looked forward to his thirteenth birthday, when he too would commence work in the coal mine. But he was unaware of the black cloud that was heading towards Senghennydd ...

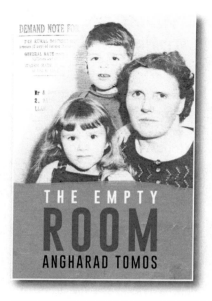

THE EMPTY ROOM
Angharad Tomos

A Welsh family's fight for a basic human right 1952-1960

£5.99

Shortlisted for the 2015 Tir na-nOg award in the original Welsh

THE IRON DAM
Myrddin ap Dafydd

A novel full of excitement and bravery about ordinary people battling for their area's future.

£5.99

Shortlisted for the 2017 Tir na-nOg award in the original Welsh

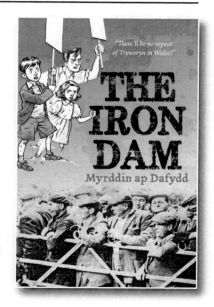

THE MOON IS RED
Myrddin ap Dafydd

Fire at a Bombing School in Llŷn in 1936 and bombs raining down on the city of Gernika in the Basque Country during the Spanish Civil War – and one family's story woven through all of this.

£6.99

Winner of the 2018 Tir na-nOg award in the original Welsh

UNDER THE WELSH NOT
Myrddin ap Dafydd

"you'll get a beating for speaking Welsh ..."

Bob starts at Ysgol y Llan at the end of the summer, but he's worried. He doesn't have a word of English. The 'Welsh Not' stigma for speaking Welsh is still used at that school.

£7.50

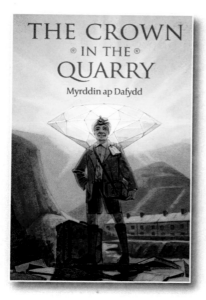

THE CROWN IN THE QUARRY
Myrddin ap Dafydd

The world's largest diamond ... in Blaenau Ffestiniog

The story of evacuees and moving London's treasures to the safety of the quarries during the Second World War.

£7

THE BLACK PIT OF TONYPANDY
Myrddin ap Dafydd

It is 1910, a turbulent time of disputes, strikes and riots in Cwm Rhondda, when the miners are fighting for fair wages and better working conditions.

People from different backgrounds are thrown together, resulting in friendships and conflict ...

£7.99

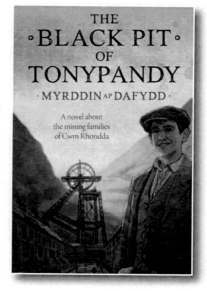

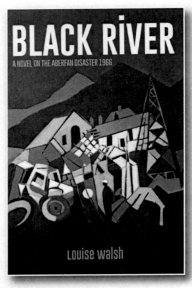

BLACK RIVER
Louise Walsh

(suitable for Young Adults)

Harry Roberts is a Cardiff journalist haunted by his failure to cover the Aberfan disaster.

Black River is a powerful piece of investigative drama that draws on the feelings of a wounded nation to show the good and bad of journalists, politicians and villagers alike.

£7.50

THE DRAGON IN THE CASTLES
Myrddin ap Dafydd

Discover the adventures of the Castles of Wales

The Holiday Blog twins – Gruff and Gwen – are visiting twenty Welsh castles. They come across strange and exciting stories – histories that are sometimes kept out of sight.

£7.50